SANS S'VILLE

SANS S'VILLE

A Series of Short Stories

ZENO FRANCIS

Brooks Becker

Copyright © 2024 by Zeno Francis

All rights reserved. No part of this book may be reproduced in any manner whatsoever without written permission except in the case of brief quotations embodied in critical articles and reviews.

This is a work of fiction. Unless otherwise indicated, all the names, characters, businesses, places, events and incidents in this book are either the product of the author's imagination or used in a fictitious manner. Any resemblance to actual persons, living or dead, or actual events is purely coincidental.

First Printing, 2024

For a friend who once gave me a book—I judged the book by its cover, and I then, regrettably, judged the book's giver. Don't judge a book by its cover, or an author by his forewords.

Contents

Dedication — v

1 Of Millersville — 1
2 Promiscuous Boy — 22
3 The Mother of Dragons — 34
4 Après in Aspen — 52
5 Photographic Memory — 70
6 A Commune in Vermont — 89
7 Make My Funk the P-Funk — 108
8 The Long Trail — 136
9 A Poignant Conclusion — 167

Notes — 193

I

Of Millersville

The sea was vast, variegated with shades of blue—and I was on a first date with one of the sea's many fishes when the idea leaped like a marlin out of water, manifested itself. The early concept was grand, but as for the execution—well, you can be the judge if you would like; just please don't be too harsh. This is my first time doing this...[1]

She was from Missouri, eight and twenty years of age. At the time, that was a year older than yours truly. Her employer was an airline, and she was an on-call flight attendant who evidently had a lot of time on her hands. She joined me for a few beers at a bar in the Graduate Hospital neighborhood of Philadelphia. The occasion went well overall—though I don't think I laughed once with much sincerity. For me, work had been hard the few days before, which has a way of slowly running down your sense of humor to a jog or walk. Fortunately, the weekend gives you just enough time to regain your comicality—you know, both your *sense* of humor and your wit, the ability to *create* humor in a timely manner. Do you agree? You might not, and that is okay.

Our discussion included surface-level topics, which was fine by me. The pessimistic person I dated before could dive down and bring me all the way to the bottom with her view on the problems of modern society. Everyone has the prerogative to analyze the organization and interplay of humanity, I suppose—even amongst the knowledgeable, there can't be two complex opinions that are the same. This type of critical chit-chat will always be good sport at the very least. You know, dignified free speech and all. Then, great minds do not necessarily think alike. Great minds engage in critical discourse like explorers attempting to discover previously unknown intellectual territory. With this previous partner, I suppose we were not compatible explorers.

With this subject, again, do you agree?[2]

We listed our interests, what we did for entertainment. We quickly chronicled the events that led us to our current, respective living situations. Our conversation remained light, she asked me what my favorite books were—answered—and then I requested she divulge parallel intelligence. The conditions were not choppy at all, really.

Like a flash of lightning on the horizon, I then crafted the chain of questions, "What if you were to write a book, what would be the style? And what would the story be about?" Positive, she was not.

But now, maybe you are starting to see—in an instant, I apparently knew—because I responded to the same question,

"The book would be about a friend of mine—*fascinating* guy—the most fascinating person I'll likely ever come to know."

* * *

From across the boardwalk many years ago, he ran toward me; excited to share the most recent event in his life. We were nineteen years old and had met only a few months before, in our first year of studying at university. Well, at least I was studying.

Ha!

Yes, in my direction, this new friend ran holding a small object mysteriously. With his hand clenched, he held his arm above his head. At first glance, I wasn't sure what the *hell* he was doing. "Hey, check out the Statue of Liberty over here!"

Earlier that evening, we drank strong liquor. The liquor was grain alcohol and 190 proof—one shot of this rectified spirit and you're immediately fighting for your senses. That summer, I was living down the shore. I had a few jobs—one was at a kiosk selling drinks, cigarettes, and compressed air advertised as pure oxygen. He was visiting the same beach town, accompanied by a group of young men from where he grew up, including another college friend—Chaz Julian. For a while, before we ventured to the boardwalk, we merrily conversed and drank light beer with ease. With more difficulty, we took shots of this liquor at the condo that they were renting for a few days. It was the summer break between our freshman and sophomore years.

The boardwalk spanned twenty or so city blocks by the ocean—several of which had a variety of stores, arcades, pizzerias, ice cream shops, amusement parks, water parks...there were a bunch of family-oriented offerings on that barrier island, and many were consolidated there on the boardwalk. We weren't interested in any of this...we were there to meet available women—well, for this age, I suppose I should say teenage girls—like a bunch of young Casanovas.

Giacomo Casanova was born in Venice. Venice was a required stop on the Grand Tour for young, upper-class men of eighteenth-century Europe. The city was a pleasure capital that tolerated social vices. Casanova was a libertine and wrote his memoir *Histoire de ma vie* as he approached death. One could argue that shamelessness is a needed condition to be romantically liberal—so, when he was my age he probably could not be bothered with reconciling events like I am trying to do. His formative years were spent in Venice. The boardwalk may have been the experimental equivalent for teenagers of the Mid-Atlantic region of the United States of America early in the twenty-first century. For on that evening, I do believe a few of us found ourselves lying in the shadows of sand dunes accompanied by cute girls to smooch.

We split up for some reason, maybe for the reason just noted. He rejoined us a while after we parted—with bright lights from the series of store marquees shining in the night, sea gulls pestering hundreds of rambling vacationers indulging in the coveted, piping-hot, oil-fried, salt-covered French fries, with a Ferris wheel slowly revolving over his shoulder all as a theatrical backdrop as he returned.

In an inebriated dream, he ran up to us. Between his thumb and pointer finger, he held his front tooth above his head like he scored a touchdown; he was holding his goddamn tooth! As he approached, he started to tell us of a mishap trying to jump over a boardwalk handrail. For anyone else, this would have been a macabre incident, but he filled the scene with hilarity...for us all to rejoice.

He then stumbled on a protruded board. Between two wooden planks, he dropped his tooth shard. We laughed as he spat out profanities from his bloody mouth. This is one of the earliest semi-lucid memories I have of Henry "Hank" Bellefonte; and this would only be the first time he would lose a front tooth.

* * *

To be true, much of what follows is speculation. For instance, I imagine that with two original, God-given front teeth, in that first year of school he was a poor student. I imagine that with an artificial lefty, in his sophomore year he was even worse.[3] He was the ringleader of a disbanded group of fraternity boys—he organized, promoted, and hosted parties alongside his housemates and fellow sig tau drop-outs—and these positions he held were of high priority, *much* higher priority than the scholastic responsibility he maintained in these years.

He was the collegian diplomat that merged these sig tau dropouts with the group I helped originate when I was at university. I lived with four friends in an apartment that quickly became—what we liked to jokingly refer to as a biohazard. To this state of alert, the living space might have really succumbed, achieved rather. When the carpet was finally in desperate need of a deep clean, the leader of our bunch, my housemate—Wayne—borrowed a heavy-duty carpet cleaner and proceeded to clean the letter "P" into the ground in commemoration of the recent World Series champions, the 2008 Philadelphia Phillies—world *fuckin'* champions!

Together, we rapidly elevated our alcohol consumption—both in terms of consumption per occasion, and frequency of occasions. We went from sharing a few cases, to sharing a beer bubble—a short-lived spherical product of Budweiser—to the eventual feasting of the half-keg. As a team, as a well-oiled machine, we would finish whatever quantity—even if the powwow took all night.

Wayne usually had a bottle of Jack Daniels fastened to his self. If he had a sheath or holster, this would surely be its occupant. In two years and via hard work, fearless leadership, and contagious determination, he would create a remarkable collection of emptied Jack Daniels bottles, completed with a little help from his friends—made for a gaudy display above our kitchen cabinets.

At our apartment, we had an open-door policy—a rule that was especially granted to our female classmates. So, just imagine this bunch of excitable young men living on their own—can you picture them? From a financial standpoint, we could have made out better—our generosity was an easy target. But for the most part, we did not mind; because in our eyes, we were glad to provide this service, especially if this charity was reciprocated down the road. With a collective reputation of being generous and welcoming, this pact was usually honored.

Yes, our haven was a service provided—please check your self-consciousness in at the door. The setting was a grassroots stage for formulated opinion, comedic expression, and general amusement for any, and all. Hank recognized the operation we had up and running near the days of its inception. For him, our social setting was a peaceful outlet to the madness he was orchestrating on the outskirts of the quaint town of Millersville in a small neighborhood known as "E-Courts."

We threw some heavily attended shindigs back then, but the small gatherings were just as enjoyable. On quite a few occasions our place was packed to the gills. My younger, though more mature sister attended the same school. Celebrating her birth in early September was surely enough reason to gather people together. You know, start the semester off strong with a sizable party. On her behalf, we were glad to host this party. But to be honest, she also formed a posse of fun and attractive girls that we were happy to accommodate.

Two years my junior, my sister was—and she will always be—a dear friend of mine. At a defunct airport, Bader Field near Atlantic City, New Jersey, the two of us saw the band Phish. As the sun neared the inland horizon, about an hour before showtime, we arrived at this barren beach and walked through Shakedown Street. Through pop-up tents and fold-up tables standing amid the ruins of a New Jersey Babylon, we shared a tiny airplane bottle of tequila in an unplanned homage to this abandoned space. Cheerfully, we drank a few beers purchased from an entrepreneurial hippy, grinning like a flight steward, in a lawn chair selling his slightly marked-up product out of a cooler. The event was on Father's Day, and the first song the band played was called "Brother." After the show, our dad picked us up; he enjoyed the encore from his car parked outside the venue, "Quinn the Eskimo," a song written by Bob Dylan in 1967.

The main act of the evening in September would be the

ceremonial presentation of a piñata. A major deliverable of that day's afternoon was the purchase of this piñata, a task assigned to Angelo and me; meanwhile, Wayne was busy using his alternative ego to purchase the alcohol for the party. *Michael Reading* was the name on the identification card gifted by his older brother.[4]

In those days, Otto and Smitty were the late risers. Otto would wake up in his stupor and not use his real voice until dinner time—sometimes I lost track of the joke, his steadfast act would make me anxious. He emerged from his room late that morning, entered our common space, and lay on the floor between the coffee table and couch. With a swirling mind, he confirmed his wellbeing after I asked him if he was alright. I then asked him what I should put on his tombstone—he requested, "Major Hangover, Bro." A deliverable for another day, and may that day be far into the future.

So, I have now, once again, introduced you to the apartment mates: Angelo, Wayne, Otto, and Smitty. I guess do your best to remember those four for now—I don't think this damn book needs an index, right?[5] The abrasive attitude can just slip out of me—so, I apologize for my tone! Angelo and I picked out a jolly piñata that day—how is that? For us all, they were simple times.

And again, the party was well attended; and time neared for the grand surprise. So, I lead my sister into my room to discuss something seemingly important. She was my confidant. This manufactured an opportunity for Angelo to hang the piñata. After our discussion, my younger sister and I entered the common space and found the hanging piñata at the center of the room—she really appreciated the gesture!

Ha!

We handed her a broom to begin the ceremony—but just when she was readying herself for the swing, the front door opened and a group of girls entered the apartment. For some unknown and insolent reason, the lead female punched and knocked down the piñata, which burst upon collision with the floor. Livid, I looked upon the unveiled candy and airplane liquor bottles dispersed at my feet. Then, with great vengeance and *furious* anger, I beheld the culprit and produced an intimate fit of rage that the folks in attendance enjoyed. Wayne later recounted, "Dude, I thought you were gonna *kill* her."[6]

Lying defeated on the floor, the piñata represented the state that the party was nearing—that is, we underestimated the turnout for the evening. We underestimated the relative amount of party stuff needed—and so, as we reached the end of the beer keg, this story's lead character—who knows, maybe you started to forget him already—arose, and he masterminded a resolution.

* * *

Yes, he resolved these dire straits with a decision—you will see—that was marked with ingenuity. While the strong are getting stronger, and the intelligent are continuously devoted to becoming more intelligent, the ingenious reveal their ingenuity in the most unexpected ways.

For the day was Saturday—the generally festive day after Friday. And on this day before—Friday—Hank had a party which followed Thirsty Thursday, a celebration of yore. I mean he was a real, modern-day Jay Gatsby of the time—and yours truly, Nick Carraway.

Similar festivities contained within the days that preceded this are plausible—the likely outcome of all of these events was that he was left with joyful memories of female companionship—and the definite outcome was that he was left with the better half of a half-keg of beer, which sat unutilized in the basement of his rented home a mile away, on the outskirts of town in a grungy community of fraternity life. We all referred to this place as "E-Courts."

"Should we go to E-Courts?" was a question one would ask with a bit of nervousness, excitement driven by possibility— one would ask this before they and their friends would agree, "Alright, let's go to E-Courts." Today, you could not pay me to go to an E-Courts party. Ehh, that's a lie. "Should we go to E-Courts?"

The answer to the problem at hand would require a logistical strategy, and you will soon understand that Hank was a resourceful young man. At this hour of the night, the half-keg sitting idly at his abode would revive the party. Hank would be the savior—he and the half-keg would extend the convivial event. The heavy aluminum cylinder simply needed to be transported from his place to ours. With our combined state of mindfulness, driving was not an option—that would have been irresponsible—and we were all under the legal age to possess and drink alcohol, so discretion in this matter was of utmost importance. To intensify the challenge we faced, in the direct route between our homes, a goddamn policeman was most certainly parked, gobbling up underage suckers like a game of Pac-Man.

●●●●●●●●●●●●●●●●●●●●●

To identify the article leveraged by Hank in his successful transport of the beer, I must take a quick step back and establish the layout of the small apartment in which I lived. On this night, the common room of our apartment was adorned with the birthday girl's piñata. Usually, the space had been laid out openly—with a few chairs and two couches. One couch was beige and sat under a large window that had vertical blinds which we slowly destroyed. At the blinds, some things were kicked, others were thrown.

The second couch was of a floral design and had been passed down to Wayne from his brother, too. Otto supplied a colorful blanket of thick thread assembled at a location that one would assume was south of the border—yes, this Mexican blanket hung on the wall above the hand-me-down couch of floral design. Decorating another wall was a tapestry which served as a message to visitors conveying our collective toleration for drug usage—uppers, downers. Two reddish-pink chairs sat in front of this tapestry, and a coffee table stood in the center of the room. A television occupied the corner opposite the kitchen, which—without division—neighbored our living room. The living room contained at least one of the apartment inhabitants at most, if not all, times. A social bunch, we were.

Wayne did not sleep much those days—he was like a damn vampire. Otto was an alcohol-induced narcoleptic. They were Yin and Yang, though Cheech and Chong was the costume Otto and Angelo wore that upcoming Halloween. Smitty and I dressed as Tweedle Dee and Tweedle Dum, a pretty authentic portrayal if I do write so myself. Wayne, a whiskey-drinking Richard Simmons—I love that crazy son of a bitch.

In addition to all these belongings, we had two chairs that bounced around the room—one called *the throne*. The throne created a figurative platform of pride for the person who had been successful in any video game we had recently played. The other chair had wheels. As I try to recollect the acquisition of this wheelchair, it is regrettably unclear—and, you know, I assume at some point someone needed this wheelchair. Nevertheless, in our apartment, inhabited by young and certainly strong individuals, we possessed a wheelchair.

My sister's party was well attended, and people were in high spirits. The piñata calamity and its dispiriting effect had quickly withered—and for those gathered, prolonging the cheerful spirits further into the evening felt imperative. Then Hank indicated mysteriously, "Carl, I got an idea."

He and Carl Magoin embarked on a quest with the wheelchair. To Hank's abode a mile away, they pushed the wheelchair. I assume at some point Hank pushed a seated Carl—and at another point, Carl pushed a seated Hank. The concrete path involved a short decline bending sharply leftward at the bottom of the hill. To use a winter sport enthusiast's expression, *bombing* this slope would have made for an extreme challenge worth attempting.

Upon their arrival and without hesitation, they hauled the half-keg up from the basement. Atop the wheelchair, the container of beer now sat—they dressed the half-keg with a coat and scarf, tucked a pair of pants under the keg, and dangled them over the front of the chair. Yes, the mission then involved pushing the seated half-keg of beer—surreptitiously dressed as a handicapped human—directly in front of law enforcement, parked there along the only logical path between the homes.

"Moment of *truth* right here, man," Hank would have shared his opinion of the situation. Maybe the copper truly did not recognize the keg being convincingly pushed along in the dark...or perhaps his withdrawal of interference was a salute to the effort of Hank and Carl. Either way, the half-keg was transferred to the party successfully—like a long-lost relative wheeled through our front door, the splendorous sight of Hank, Carl, and the beer made for a fantastic goddamn laugh and much cheer.

With the keg finally tapped, Smitty poured beer into our plastic cups—this was his duty, and when mine was filled to the brim, Smitty smoothly transferred the flow to the next cup, held by Hank. After I immediately took a swig, he sagaciously imparted, "Woah, you gotta cherish that, dude."

Looking him in the eyes, I said, "When you're right, you're right." But with beer nearing the top of his cup, he did not quite wait for Smitty to make the first move. He quickly raised the cup to his mouth and chugged away. "You fucker," I snickered and then joined him, consuming the foamy beer without pause.

On the third day a wedding took place at Cana in Galilee. Jesus' mother was there, and Jesus and his disciples had also been invited to the wedding. When the wine was gone, Jesus' mother said to him, "They have no more wine." "Woman, why do you involve me?" Jesus replied. "My hour has not yet come." His mother said to the servants, "Do whatever he tells you." Nearby stood six stone water jars, the kind used by the Jews for ceremonial washing, each holding from twenty to thirty gallons. Jesus said to the servants, "Fill the jars with water," so they filled them to the brim. Then he told them, "Now draw some out and take it to the master of the banquet." They did so, and the master of the banquet tasted the water that had been turned into wine. He did not realize where it had come from, though the servants who had drawn the water knew. Then he called the bridegroom aside and said, "Everyone brings out the choice wine first and then the cheaper wine after the guests have had too much to drink; but you have saved the best till now." What Jesus did here in Cana of Galilee was the first of the signs through which he revealed his glory; and his disciples believed in him.[7]

* * *

Tired? Hungover? If you needed refreshing for ailments of any sort, I recommended flavored oxygen from a kiosk in the Surf Mall in Ocean City, New Jersey. I also collected money on behalf of an artist who airbrush-painted names onto hats, license plates, and shirts. During a shift, the artist smoked many cigarettes and would breathe in the cloudy hue of paint he created by his airbrush instrument. He carried with him a terrible cough and had glazed, film-coated eyes. His labor was an odd sacrifice that I pitied him for...but he spoke of the late nineties fondly, like he had been the lead singer of a touring rock band.

During the day, I worked as a lifeguard at the waterpark on Brigantine Avenue. Behind my sunglasses, I closed my eyes and vigilantly swiveled my head in the formation of spokes on the top half of a bicycle. My favorite station was the top of the Serpentine ride—the vantage there might have been the best in Ocean City. "Alright, go," feigning grumpiness just for the hell of it, pointing down the watery ramp indicating a rider's permission to slide.

"Go?" a little one would ask. "Yes, go! I said go!" for Chrissake. The next kid would step up to the starting point, jets blasting on his heels, piss running down his leg.

For three years, I worked at Gumper's Island. Hank and his misbehaving friends were the only hooligans I recall getting thrown out of the waterpark. Prior to the terminus of Serpentine, there was a circular pool raised about twenty feet above ground. An inner-tube rider would eventually dump into this pool in the sky, and a lifeguard would escort a rider to the final slide. If I was stationed there, I would act like a foreigner from my own made-up nation, and practice a fabricated foreign accent, "You want spin?" But I was stationed in the lazy river, and the Serpentine pool was in front of me.

On Hank and company's second ride down the Serpentine, they ditched the tubes over the fence surrounding the sky pool, overwhelmed the lifeguard, and rode the final plummet standing like surfers on their feet. One of them slipped and landed flush on his back—like an overturned beetle flailing the rest of the way down the slide. I watched from the lazy river and let out a crooked smiled while holding the whistle in my teeth.

During high school, my friends and I, also like toppled and helpless beetles, were not highly mobile. In a suburban town outside of Philadelphia, we enjoyed our isolation, and were aware of—but couldn't explain—our naivety. Otto and Angelo attended my high school, and we were the three compadres. Our journey to a rock concert at the Wilmington Opera House in Delaware—thirty minutes south of our hometown—was a huge undertaking. As fortunate high school seniors, Otto and I hitched a ride with five attractive girls into Philadelphia to see a funk band called Bodega.[8] Julia drove us to World Café Live in the city in style—that is, we arrived in her mother's child-lock enabled minivan. And to get to Millersville, Otto, Angelo, and I drove west like pioneers in wagons.

The hamlet of Millersville was located within the adjacent county of Lancaster. We drove on Route 30 for a half an hour—after exiting the highway at a town called Gap, the rest of the roads carved in and out of grassy fields and farmland. On this route, we were certain to pass by an Amish family riding a horse and buggy, or a young Amish child kicking along on a scooter. Yes, we would definitely pass a few parties of Amish on a single ride to Millersville.

Route 741 reached an intersection with a farmstand called Cherry Hill Orchards. "Take a right turn at the traffic light there," and the excitement started to set in—you are getting close. Bending around the bottom of a hill in your automobile, turning slowly left to come upon another farmstand on the right side of the road, with an affordable offering that did not experience inflation—two dollars for a dozen ears of corn. Getting back in the car, driving onward and upward, to the top of one more of the rolling hills to the vista of the nearby water tower of Millersville—signs change from Route 741 to a more natural identity, Millersville Road.

"There will be a cemetery on the left, that's when you take a left at the next intersection...onto Manor Avenue," your guide instructed. Small businesses serving Millersville Marauders begin cropping up like stalks of corn—barbers, delicatessens, the John Herr's Village Market that accepted the special, parentally funded financial account called Marauder Gold. "Then you take a left turn at Penn Manor Beverage," the sole beer distributor in town. On George Street, you would finally arrive at this college town.

As you crossed Cottage Avenue, academic buildings became the new crop. Unharvested, the retro sign that read "Sugar Bowl" was to the left. Looking down the road, you passed along slowly in backed-up traffic leading to the main intersection of town. At the end of the road, you would catch a glimpse of the Sugar Bowl pizza restaurant—and there was McPherson Stadium further off in the distance, the home of the winless football team.

Passing the old red-brick library to your right, a sidewalk veered down a hill to a gazebo, to a small pond with swans, willow trees, and the mathematics building all radiant in the light of day. Driving along to the intersection of Frederick Street, rather than driving through to the center of campus—which contained dining halls, classroom buildings, and freshman dormitories—you rotated the wheel clockwise hand over hand, the Meters' "Cissy Strut" sounding out your rolled-down windows. You were attempting to turn scholarly heads. Suddenly, you had gone off campus, where many of the apartments were located—Wellington Apartments, Brook & Timber Apartments, the apartment complex on Duke Street.

Only a few places to buy a draft beer in Millersville—the

House of Pizza was up the hill on Frederick Street. On Thursdays, you could sing karaoke and buy a light beer for fifty cents. Down the road from the House of Pizza was Baker's Tavern—stop there for chicken wings or a steak tip sandwich —play a tune from the juke box; just don't choose "Brandy" by Looking Glass because Wayne played that every time we were there. He played the song for the bartender with the resplendent rear end, her name was—you guessed it—Brandy.

Prince Street took you to Hillview Avenue, which brought you back closer to campus again, to Shenks Lane—alright enough with the goddamn roads and directions. In the shadows of the Student Memorial Center, you began to circle around campus. We explored behind Suliman Gymnasium— walked through the woods behind the building where the Conestoga River flows south to the Susquehanna.

"You want to swim across?" dared Hank.

"Sure, why not—" a few of us dropped down to our skivvies and swam to the other side. The mud was gross, felt and faintly smelled like shit from fertilized farmland. We looked up the river and saw an abandoned aluminum boat, swam over, and commandeered the vessel. We gave her a clever name like *S.S. Tits*. Floated along for a few hundred feet—eventually running aground into rocks with no way to steer. We needed a lifeguard to push us down the slide while we kicked and splashed our feet, "You want spin?"

As a lifeguard, I would drowsily revolve my head like a damn water sprinkler. Glanced up to find the silhouette of Hank, standing at the top of the Serpentine sky pond, casting a shadow with blue skies and fluffy clouds above him. Like a damn Frisbee, he launched his inner tube across the heavens.

Right foot in front of the left, he scooched forward and surfed down the slide.

"Hey, you can't do that!" cried out another lifeguard. With arms extended outward for balance, he neared the part of the slide that smoothed out for landing into the final pool. He jumped at the end, alighted into the water holding a knee in the can-opener form. Whistles blowing like mad, his splash subsided, he emerged fast from the waves that he cast, belting a "Woo!" loudly for all parkgoers to hear.

* * *

Hank Bellefonte was the catalyst that brought together two groups of young men. At first, we were unaware of our similar perspectives, shared intents. Hank studied biology, and I understand "catalyst" to be some kind of scientific expression, so for this circumstance the word has been ironically borrowed. You should know these are *my* stories, or I guess *our* stories since you have now become engrossed in what I have to say. Hey, this doesn't seem like "usual mindless boring getting to know you chit-chat."[9] For the sake of structure, I will highlight my understanding of Hank's forging of a unique version of young adulthood which I considered worth telling —my forging might be worth telling, too. I am not recounting tales of tribulation, then rectification leading to triumph. This isn't historical fiction that is riddled with humor. There will be no wizards, or anything fantastical, for that matter.

If you are into literary prognostication—or if you would like some sort of indication as to what you are getting yourself into here—if you have read JD Salinger's *Catcher in the Rye* and *Nine Stories* or F. Scott Fitzgerald's *The Great Gatsby*, maybe saddle up for a novella that is akin to these masterpieces. When I realized to whom Holden Caulfield was telling his story, I broke down in goddamn tears.

With Hank, I never fell too far to the wayside over the years and was even able to collect what I believe is a noteworthy series of stories; they will cover a decade of memories. So now you know, this first story of Millersville was the sturdy foundation for the following pages, albeit a wheelchaired foundation. This next short story is less foundational—really embarking on our tale here, little by little. I hope you enjoy.

> When Hank was a child, he was the main suspect in an incident of chalk-graffiti; that is, a daring classmate wrote the word "FUCK" in chalk at recess. Hank took the blame even though he was not the true perpetrator. His mother still stays, "I can't believe you did that, why would you do that, Hank?" to which he always replies, "I know, Mom, I'm a real piece of shit!"

A commendation to her anniversary of vaginal evacuation is what Hank bid to my sister on that fateful evening many years ago—everyone else just said, "Happy Birthday!" His primary craft was his method with words—though vulgarity would be one's immediate interpretation. But as his phrases were stated so plainly, and were often inarguable, he provided his listener—during quick digestion of his axioms or general remarks such as this previous example—first, a subtle feeling of astonishment. Then, a sense of elucidation in his unconventional interpretation of things. But most importantly, these types of statements led to shared laughter.

Two millennia ago, Jesus Christ salvaged the festive nature on an evening in Cana in Israel. My fascinating friend —Henry "Hank" Bellefonte—lengthened the jubilant spirits conjured on this evening, in this chapter of life—in this quaint town of Millersville.

2

Promiscuous Boy

His physical appearance and choice of wardrobe were a matter of intrigue. Yes, without shame or fear that you will construe me as a person of homosexual tendency—not that that is a shameful sexual preference that one should avoid expressing—I found his physical presence to be, you know, pretty goddamn intriguing. And based on his record with women, I understand that a considerable portion of women would also agree with this notion, and maybe even consider him handsome in a way.

Yes, I suppose he was a handsome young dude—built stout and of moderate height—standing at about the length of a fathom. Grew out his hair in those first few years at Millersville, eventually sported a lion's mane that hung just short of his shoulders. Dirty blond hair with a full, brown beard—all in all, the likeness of a mountain man. A commonly worn garment was a flannel shirt, mindfully unbuttoned—because in his closet, a great arsenal of ridiculous shirts waited...each too worthy of presentation to conceal with a *buttoned* flannel shirt.

"As long as your shoes don't squeak, you're dressed well in my book," he would say.

Some shirts were simple—featuring portraits of a fish, bear, or cat—and others were intricate; for instance, a shirtless Native American riding a unicorn amid a purple-hued cloud before a rainbow. In the winter, his clothing was sturdier and threaded into tribal patterns. His raiment was unbranded even though he would refer to himself on occasion as a *basic bitch*. He ultimately achieved the look of a grungy hippy who had stepped down from mountains—peaks, valleys, and cliffs of which he had sought and found many thrills. I thought this complemented the nature of his personality well—his sartorial look was no guise or ruse.

I was on track to graduate from college in four years—Hank Bellefonte took the five-year path for the same accomplishment. "Five years, icing on the cake some may say...a sixth year would be like dumping sugar straight from the box," he justified.

To our respective hometowns we returned upon graduation as fresh products for the labor market—eager to dismantle corporate formalities. Hank and Angelo held down the fort after many of us left; I returned to the fort a few times that following school year. Hank became a better student then, setting aside adequate consciousness to be put toward academics—but partying, partaking in adventures with his friends, and stirring up sexual conquests would remain his primary objectives. The fort may have been infiltrated, or those in charge were getting wackier; or, worse, with each homecoming I had conformed more to the mild, professional lifestyle. Yes, the collegiate aura seemed more outlandish every time I went back to visit my alma mater. Like a ship fading away from the harbor, I lamented my former self, with cargo too heavy to turn back.

* * *

With all this pondering and writing, maybe we'll answer a few questions. During the age that's been thus far referenced, are standalone promiscuous happenstances more easily excused? Will this be the general state of the human sexual experience, with two periods in life that a person generally experiences? That is, there is an experimental, juvenile age and a more developed one. Eventually, we are cast into established young adults, married or unmarried, greater in mortal years and, perhaps, in morality. Guilt or remorse in casual sexual interaction does not seem to carry the same weight at younger ages—otherwise stated, the idea of sexual exhibition driven by pure lust may have a stronger pull than the tug of pending guilt. You know, the dishonorable aftermath of sex without any greater intention—otherwise stated, sometimes college students just fuck and continue with their social lives the least awkwardly as possible.

Attempting this explanation was an uncomfortable task, and perhaps it was a prudish assessment. In yesteryear, there were swingers. Today, there are outwardly proclaimed polygamists and polyamorists, and a variety of genders or sexualities from which one is free to choose. An esteemed author and social critic with the stylized pen name of bell hooks—

no need to capitalize names—more eloquently elaborated on a similar matter:

> *Approaching romantic love from a foundation of care, knowledge and respect actually intensifies romance. By taking the time to communicate with a potential mate we are no longer trapped by the fear and anxiety underlying romantic interactions that take place without the discussion of the sharing of intent and desire.*[10]

Chock full o' insight, bell hooks broadly discussed love. I left the book on top of my crapper, and I'd read a page or two per visit. Take a look while you're in there, but please don't forget to put the lid down when you're done. I don't want your damn fecal matter spraying all over the place.

It's a good book. On promiscuity, I guess hooks would excuse a one-night stand—but according to this passage, she would argue that transparency, rather than deception and feigned interest, would improve the intensity of the romantic interaction—which sort of sounds like an ideal scenario. Or yet again—and more aligned to my theory—at this age, maybe these matters are best left unarticulated.

Sleeping around ultimately leaves one with a reputation known at some hierarchal level of the great social network. But this standing was never much of a concern for Hank Bellefonte. His indifference to judgment fortunately makes these tales fairly tell-able. He ultimately fashioned a steady relationship with a girl that resembled Khaleesi from the popular HBO show *Game of Thrones*. Towards the end of my experience at university, she entered into the picture. I observed their relationship sporadically during my later visits. For as great of a catch as she might have been—Khaleesi was a bombshell—Hank did not seem to have any challenge with her wooing. In the complicated hunt, sometimes romantic matches occur effortlessly; they are almost melodramatic.

Hank had a dog named Bertha. Khaleesi may have been smitten by Hank as he rolled through campus, pulled by the beautiful pit bull mastiff. Bertha was named after the popular tune by the Grateful Dead. She would yank him along (the dog, that is) as he wore roller skates, yelling, "Woo fucking woo!" as a quick activity between classes.

Quite the large dog, Bertha grew to become. It was bound to happen given her breed. Destined for greatness, you could see this in her fixed countenance, in her anthropomorphic demeanor. She was the second dog in the house, succeeded a dog whose tenancy did not last very long. Black Floyd—another musical homage paid via naming convention—was a troublesome pit bull of black coloration, with a tail that wagged at an inopportune height, constantly knocking into objects placed on the coffee table. Despite difficulties at the onset of the relationship between the dog and his new owners—such as this problematic disregard for coffee table objects, or personal space more generally—Black Floyd started to show indications of decency. He was becoming more dutiful and respectful. At the time of procurement, he seemed to be an incurably bad dog. *"Who's a bad dog, you's a bad dog, Black Floyd!"*

As housemates, Hank, Stan Green, and Jim Shelley acquired the dog from a group of girls that were living across the street. The housemates observed that these previous owners treated him poorly. In the basement, the dog was stowed away, and was fed cereal, for Chrissake—what a cruel situation. The girls were taking care of him on behalf of a guy they knew who was in prison. For a few months, he was locked up for a crime this writer does not recall. Magnanimously, Hank, Stan, and Jim offered to overhaul the caregiving responsibilities from these ladies. An act of justice, as they would not sit idly by as the innocent dog suffered a punishment similar to its incarcerated owner.

We broke bread on karaoke night. That is, a group of us—including these female companions—occupied two circular tables at the House of Pizza. The fifty cent light beers were our treat—the plastic cup pyramid was growing taller by the minute—and the Ho-Pie employees were getting angry. Hank was purchasing the next round of beers when Jim placed a cup at the apex of the pyramid. The manager asked Hank to tell Jim to "take those cups down," to which he replied, "Why don't you tell him yourself?" The manager then marched over and kicked Jim out of Ho-Pie. Exiting the restaurant, Jim banged on the glass windows as he heel-kick skipped from left to right—what a poorly behaved group of gentlemen.

And yes, after a rough, poorly behaved start, Black Floyd was beginning to show some upside. The quality of his manner was improving. But on one occasion, Black Floyd foolishly meddled with a skunk and was sprayed—lit up by the stinky skunk stuff. *Try to say those three words a few times and fast out loud, I dare ya...especially if you are reading this book in public...could benefit from the advertisement!*

During a party, Hank took the pit bull out for an evening perambulation to do his business. Among the attendees, there were a few girls who were—you know—interested in Hank and his housemates. In those promiscuous times, these girls would pretty assuredly find themselves sharing-the-sheets-so-to-speak of Hank, Stan, or Jim. After the confrontation with the skunk, Hank took Black Floyd back to the house and brought him directly to the bathroom up the stairs. Hastily passing through the living room was all the time needed to fully stink up the place, clear out the party, and permanently contribute to the stench of the home—a seemingly terminal aroma. Everyone evacuated, including the girls—an evening of unfulfilled romance.

"That fuckin' dog, man...we were getting laid for sure!" vowed Stan, who was most excited about the promising sexual situation. Jim was immediately concerned about the new level of rank the house had reached. "We gotta do something about this—I've got tomato juice, that's the move, *right*?" Jim would have paused the nonsense and pushed for a solution.

"Yeah—and I have garlic...don't worry, I'll take care of this." Hank dropped down to his skivvies, brought the dog up the stairs, hopped into the shower after taking off his last garment, and got to scrubbing the dog with the concoction. Making up a melody, he sang for all to hear, "Black Floyd...you *stinky*, stinky dog!"

Jim interrupted at last, "What the fuck is he doing with garlic?" I'll never know. Weeks later, the convict returned from prison. He reclaimed the dog from their possession. Black Floyd moved back in with his original owner and his grandmother. Black Floyd quickly settled back into old ways—habits the grandmother with her precious years to live could not handle—and she decided to put the dog down.

Black Floyd—maybe the lamb of God who was sacrificed so that, despite our sins, we could live forever...but seriously, this was an unfortunate story that I was sorry to tell. So it goes—a sad storyline.[11]

* * *

The lamb of God paved the way for the coming of Bertha, whose obedient manner was an element of her blessed instincts. To my knowledge, she did not need much behavioral training from Hank or his fellow housemates. Vision to a blind man in Bethsaida, cleaned a man of leprosy once he returned from the mountain, water to wine for a celebration in Cana—perhaps this all occurred—and practically speaking, Alexander the Great created the communication network for the gospel to spread to the civilized humans of the time; yes, otherwise, Jesus Christ would have been merely a local phenomenon. As it pertains to Hank and his miracles, this work could perhaps be referred to as the gospel according to Zeno. I implore others to spread the good word.

Despite the unwelcoming scent, their place took over headquartering responsibilities at Millersville—this tale's Jerusalem. There were a lot of reasons why their house cast an uninviting smell; eventually—for instance—they would raise young chickens and turkeys from the basement. They were concerned for Black Floyd when he was banished to the basement. I suppose this comparable, ornithological arrangement could be viewed as cruel—though for the folks that witnessed the coop, the operation was hilarious. From ground level, they first asked, "What the *hell* is going on down there?"

With the pungent odor of chicken shit exuding upward

to the home's main level, the coop would become an obvious cause of the home's strange scent. Prior to the coop, the unkempt basement was already a gaseous, musty space. But these housemates were not to blame—the circumstance was the result of decades of neglect common to those properties, stacked side by side on Elizabeth Court. Carl, Angelo, and I dealt with a similar scent across the street—contributing further to the irreversible feculence was the only option.[12]

Tacked to the wall, a slice of American-style cheese contributed to the odor of Hank's home, too. The artwork was too fastened to the wall to be removed. The preservative content of those dairy products must be extreme because that thing aged considerably well. The room was surely at an unrefrigerated temperature. The slice of cheese never grew mold. It just slowly curled up and away from the wall on its cheese slice edges, a goddamn mystery...

Fastened to the living room ceiling, an ornate sequence of adhesive tape drooped so to capture flies. Those dangling fly tapes eventually collected an outstanding number, were flat-out covered. Positioned above the coffee table in the middle of the room, a distinct roll of fly tape was placed. This roll was central to an anecdote that will disclose to you—if you didn't already know—this group's stance on psychedelic drugs. Many happenings in this home were influenced by the use of pot and alcohol, but heavier drugs found their way into circulation from time to time—supplementing collective decision-making, philosophical realizations, and joke-telling abilities. And of all the happenings, one of the strangest was architected by Carl's hometown friend. He was known as

The Master, and he visited on one particularly stimulating evening.

From his seat on the sofa, emerging from a long period of quietness, The Master stood on the coffee table. He drew his intrigued face a foot from the fly tape. This action alone captured the attention of all the folks in the crowded room—and at ease, as if a fly were a raisin in a box, he picked one from the adhesive strip.

"Yo, check this out!" Hank summoned the kitchen dwellers. There he stood—The Master atop the coffee table. The first fly, with a twitching, free wing, must have felt saved for a moment—the Master and Savior. Released from its slow world of doom and despair. Before, the fly was imprisoned, trapped on the tape, and left to die as a symbol—a warning for other flies to fly in a different home. This first fly was detached—then The Master brought the specimen to his mouth, and he ate the fly!

The abnormality of this decision was a damn riot. There he stood on the coffee table with everyone in the room laughing. I had my hands on my damn knees, was hunched over and hysterical, "Can you believe he just ate that fly!" We were crying, for Chrissake.

Despite the hysteria, his countenance went unchanged, was like a concerned culinary critic—curious, quizzical even, as he looked upon the fly tape he considered the flavor of the fly. His countenance transitioned to one of glee like the expression of a toddler during a simple discovery. Then, unrelentingly, he continued the feast! The Master made a meal out of the spread of flies—slowly chewing, working on the tape at a pace of perhaps a fly every ten seconds. Yes, from the sumptuous fly tape, he ate and eventually had his virtuosic fill—a savant on the frontline of culinary exploration. To a seat on the couch, he returned, satisfied with the performance.

* * *

This fly tape—placed in the middle of the room, positioned above the coffee table, central to this former anecdote—may unveil to you the stance on psychedelic drugs maintained by some of these young scholars. Going forward, drugs do not need much recognition for any actions and decisions made by the lead character, or his companions; this is not a supernatural, drug-induced experiment to Las Vegas. But I'll evoke a sense of finality by offering a statement by a student who would later attend our alma mater, who would find his way into the local news for indecent exposure. That is, he undressed and jumped naked on a car, one occupied by a policeman. "College is for tripping on drugs," is what he had to say to the news reporter. I was so surprised to find that in the paper. Where is that editor now? I could use an editor.[13]

With the odor of the home, Bertha did not seem to have much of an issue. Khaleesi did not seem to mind the odor either. She frequently attended parties and grew to be an amusing addition to the group, along with her posse. She implemented a sense of humor reminiscent of Hank and his comicalness—adopted his aptitude in unique naming conventions, an example being her car which she called Thunder Goose, or her dog who was named Mudd.

Like Bertha, at first she did not mind the drug use. Over time, I understand this attitude changed. Across a stretch of time, there are a lot of changes—though sometimes change does not need much time at all—one night goes awry and you fall from grace. Make a wrong decision, like a wave during high tide, washing away a castle you thought was safe from the sea. When I start getting overly poetic, wrapping up feels prudent. How long ago were you a student off at school? Five years ago? Ten? Wow, have *twelve* years really passed?

What if we met then? At university, with all our potential. Naïve, pure, but maybe starting to tarnish, preparing for our corruption; or maybe we could age honorably. Driving home on holiday, thinking one of us could someday be the president of the damn country.

3

The Mother of Dragons

"Why is he so interesting?" In earnest, she wondered from across the table, still assessing if her date was interesting as well—the girl from Missouri, that is. She and I would have a second rendezvous. After that, a third. Summarizing, I told her how his accounts with women, his unique employment choices, and the stories that consequently arose from his line of work were all reasons—but more generally, his adventurous spirit made him fit to be the lead character of a story. I will try, but not doing him justice feels unavoidable. This gospel according to Zeno will likely be insufficient.

I suppose there could have been a fourth date and a fifth date with the girl from Missouri. On a Saturday evening, I went to a concert with Hank and Ike Isaac. We saw a jam band called Lotus. Earlier that day, I snowboarded at the Poconos with a few of my housemates. We traveled an hour north, to Bear Creek Mountain, out the door before the sun rose that morning, and quickly arrived at that glorified hill. We parked the car, first row from the entrance.

And the evening before I was with the flight attendant from Missouri. She served me a delicious cabbage and beef soup. Sacrilegiously, there was no grace spoken prior to the meal—that's right, we ate like a couple of cats in a damn alley. After, we watched a movie and played with her cats. Shortly before midnight, I took my leave. She put my coat on for me after she clumsily tied my shoes. As she was tying them, I was not sure what to make of the gesture. During the ride home I reflected on the service and decided that, regardless of her inelegance, she surely performed a kind deed.

In the darkness, before the dawn, I woke up after a short duration of sleep. With haste, we set forth to the slopes.[14] I pensively drank coffee while looking upon the flashing of earth tone colors out the window, from the backseat, behind the driver. I finished the coffee while I put on my boots in the parking lot. I drank the last sip from the travel mug, and then cracked open a beer. While we waited for the opening of the lift ticket office, we had a few beers for breakfast. In the meantime, we wondered if we could hike up the mountain. The driver developed celiac disease, identified the issue years later—one of the last rounds of beer I recall having with this friend. As I presently narrate our former selves and the giant steps we took, our boozy morning itinerary brings me cheer.

Snow sports such as snowboarding can be quite tiring. I followed this full-day recreational activity with a dance party that lasted until two o'clock in the morning. The band was named Lotus, as you may recall despite my rambling. Hank, Ike Isaac, a bunch of goddamn hippies, and I danced around like hippy hooligans; and as the concert was ending, I brazenly requested the girl from the Midwest come over and join me for the night's slumber. When I returned home, I received a fortuitous message that confirmed she could accompany me, "I'll be there in ten minutes." She was out at a bar in my neighborhood.

Well, I woke up at nine o'clock the next day with my phone in my hand. "Shit, shit, *shit*!" I exclaimed, starting the day. Please forgive me, God, but I wasn't mad because I missed church. Yes, I fell asleep prior to her arrival, and I messaged her back in the morning. She told me that she waited outside for a little while—then she figured I had fallen asleep. I should have sat up and made myself a glass of water, or left the door unlocked; though my felonious urban neighbors may have entered in her stead.

Later that afternoon, I met up with Hank and Ike. On a renascent scooter—a two-wheeled vehicle from my childhood, stowed in my parents' garage for many years—I rode over to Ike's neck of the concrete woods, to the Passyunk area of South Philadelphia. I am a tall person and aboard my scooter, with its puny wheels fit for a child or teenager, I appeared especially large. Just a few months before, the inaugural scooter ride to Ike's house occurred with a prank. I called Ike when I was approaching, "Ah dude, you have to come outside…someone *fucked up* your car!" I then went into a full-power, high-speed scooter stride—arrived, hauling ass down his street at the same time he busted out of his rented home—I rapidly shifted his moods with this trick I played.

We recounted the previous evening. I told them of my foolishness. Hank advised, "Dude, that's hilarious…just don't do that again! That'll be the end of your little relationship...because chicks don't give you two chances with that type of shit." For lunch, we anchored our elbows at a couple bars near Ike's place and had a few beers—then we picked up some ingredients for a meal of pasta and fresh scallops that Hank reeled in from a recent trip at sea. I had another beer while we cooked our early dinner—four in all for the day...maybe five.

As I digested, I invited the girl from Missouri over once more, and she accepted—but warned me to not fall asleep this go-around. But, with the taxing events from the day before, and the improper recovery on this Sunday, I was just so exhausted. Belly up in my bed, I woke up at around midnight—so ashamed of my folly. Yet again, I fell asleep before she arrived. In my late-night stupor, I then called her...and with a disenchanted tone, she answered one last time.

***

On that Monday, I had a busy day of work—was probably for the best that she did not join me in slumber as I would have been even more sluggish. That evening's dream was very supernatural and brought me to an odd state of semi-consciousness. I believe the name of this phenomenon is sleep paralysis.

Under Otto's Mexican rug that hung on the wall—dreaming myself back to university—I lay on the couch. In my dream, I slept on the couch—which transported me to a new place of my current slumber...immediately weird. As I drifted to sleep, my mind and consciousness were violently sucked down by some black mass—the imagery was terrifying. In my chest, I felt a terrible sensation. As I was pulled downward, I was pleading to God, "God, I'm trying to believe in you...I'll try to believe in you...please, God, I believe in you."

"I believe in you!" I tried.

"God, I *love* you!" with more conviction.

As I pled my case to the Almighty One, rays of light shined from above, and defended me from this darkness that sought to have me plummet to the depths of Earth, or to some other place altogether. "God, I believe in you! God, I love you!"

I snapped away from this demonic mass. In a lovely feeling of calm relief, I sat up to find a female that I had been with prior to the girl from Missouri. There had been a handful of women in between the two—but she was the last one that had been somewhat serious. She sat on the other couch at my college apartment staring at me—she was sexy, naked underneath the blanket from my bed. She stood up, "Are you ready to go back to sleep?" I rose up, walked over to her, hand on her hip, fingers from the other hand caressing her chin—I used to be so goddamn romantic. We kissed, then went to my room.

The door closed. More certainly, I awoke in Philadelphia. Her tone was disenchanted, I got out of bed feeling like a confused wizard that lost his goddamn wand.

* * *

The parting with the girl from Missouri was sort of embarrassing, an overall loss—but she was not going to be *the one* anyway. For a while, I thought that the Mother of Dragons would be the one for the Hankster—a handful of pals might have agreed with me on this prophecy. She attracted an engaging community of people, had a respectable taste in music, was outdoorsy, and was very pretty. You could say she was a shining light for the man after a dark, unpleasant experience with a girl he called the Black Widow. Victoria was the name given to her at birth. As I write with the intent to convey chronology, she may have been the first girl he had been with after he dislodged his tooth many years ago. He ran toward us in an inebriated dream...a dream ever since.

Hank and the Black Widow began their relationship while Wayne, Smitty, Otto, Angelo, and I were stirring up fun times at 57 Wellington, the thriving address of our apartment. Hank and the Black Widow were neighbors—drugs and sex were adhesive, constantly bringing them together. She put together an irrefutable offer for the guy—she possessed both strong abilities in the bedroom, and a generous supply of drugs. Frequently, the offering brought him back to her door —together, they spent many of their evenings.

"Dude—she's a *freak*," he stated when asked about her sexual nature. He would explain further with seriousness in his eyes. For about two years, they would enjoy this sexual relationship—the first of which could be considered cordial. For the most part, their time spent together was behind closed doors. The extent of their socializing would be in living rooms, often alongside her fellow sorority sisters and a friend of Hank's named Fleary. He was also dating an accomplice of the Black Widow.

Picture a night sky with stars—picture one home in the middle of a row below the sky—picture a room upstairs with the blinds drawn, a purplish hue from inside—you see two figures collapse to the bed. After this round of sex, they shared a customary cigarette. Lying there naked, and after a bit of satiated silence, Hank reached for ChapStick on the end table. He rubbed the wax on his testicles for a bit of mirth, "Ooooh yeah, that's *nice*!" They laughed first—then Victoria called him strange, so strange. So, he straddled her, grabbed her arm and then her waist, to display his strength, to create that giddy, sexual atmosphere that comes with physical vulnerability. With her free hand, she found the ChapStick in the sheets and shoved the little tube up her vagina, "Are you gonna get this out of me, you bad boy?"

So he went fishing. The line went limp, the fish seemed to have vanished. He tried to get the ChapStick out, but he struggled. The two of them spent an hour trying to extract that little tube. To make matters worse, the Black Widow had a boyfriend at the time, and this object would be an odd, but sure giveaway that she was being unfaithful. Yes, Hank was a secretive intimate friend of hers, and this evening—like many others—was a covert rendezvous.

So, to get serious in this wild operation, she snorted a painkiller of some sort. With a force that caused her to bleed, they removed the tube; it was as if she gave birth to the damn ChapStick. According to Hank, her poor crotch bled for a whole week, for Chrissake.

* * *

And, retrospectively, this relationship was one of which he was not exceedingly proud. He told me this chapped tale years later in Philadelphia. He had gone rock climbing earlier that day. We were going out in the city. Lotus was the name of the band, as you may recall. He stopped at my place first to take a shower. Provided a towel, informed him which shampoo was mine, and I made sure he had his beer with him—he chortled, "What, do you think this is my first shower?" Then he guffawed.

We got to talking about this book, these stories generally. He offered me this private, semi-erotic anecdote of the Black Widow, one that I had never heard. Hank would attribute his later heavy drug use to her *baiting* him, which went on for months. After their relationship had reached the duration of a school semester, they would persistently have jealous fights —bouts roused by the fact that they never confirmed any exclusivity. He was perfectly fine with moving on after some of their arguments—but a week would pass and she would *reel* him in with the same offer—drugs and angry, hot sex.

At the end of the tunnel, there was light. The light of summer vacation, the few months between his junior and senior years. A special name for this time akin to *Rumspringa* should be created—the fanciful conclusion of young adults being useless sons of bitches, the culmination of the fantastic collegiate party that stands on a foundation of limited responsibility. Hank just had to endure her violence until the school year ended. When it finished—all exams aced, every presentation smoothly delivered—he safely returned home to Newtown in Bucks County, Pennsylvania.

As he worked as a greenskeeper at a golf course, drugs had become a stable part of his daily routine...*come on, bark like a dog for me.*[15] Despite heavier drug use than that to which he was previously accustomed, his life was peaceful, under control. Then—on one summer day, with phone in hand, swiping right on dating applications like a madman in the greenskeeper shed, hidden from the sun—he received an invitation to join a family vacation. The invitation was extended by the Black Widow. On a whim, he accepted.

"All things considered, the trip went well," he recounted when he returned from the shower. But clearly, being his later self, with twenty-twenty hindsight, he told me he was never happy having her as a mate. Once this was realized, he dishonored himself with each new day that he led her on...sullied her and her dignity as well, I suppose. "Can I use some deodorant? Nothing cool about being stinky," he requested. I acquiesced. "Speed Stick? Twenty-four-hour protection, my ass...come on, Zeno, get yourself some Old Spice, for the love of God." He applied the deodorant. He continued weaving his tale of the Black Widow...

...Through the tunnel, to summer vacation, she graduated that semester and was not returning to the university as a student. When we resumed school in what was my final year, he straightened things out with the Black Widow. With much time to ponder—as he sculpted the immaculate scenery of the country club fairways, roughs, and greens—he realized that the time had come for him to cut the bait. He had to move on, fish somewhere else...and that was all there was to it—our insane relationship's over, that's what he told her.

* * *

Soon after, Hank began seeing a girl named Lauren. He referred to her as the Tarantula. I did not know the Black Widow very well—the Tarantula, I knew a bit better. He was introduced to her at one of the parties hosted by the Dudes of 57 Wellington. She accompanied my sister—was a classmate friend of hers, and they lived in the same dormitory as freshmen.

She was given the name Tarantula on a sickly evening. She had too much to drink, which led to her vomiting in one of our toilets—what an uncouth generation, the whole lot of us. Hank walked in on her as she was spewing—he thought her form was like that of a spider, the way she huddled around the toilet. So, Lauren—such an innocent and adorable name—was now known as the Tarantula.

To what extent Lauren hunted I am not sure, but she once killed a goddamn moose—what an astounding accomplishment. With the moose meat, Lauren and Hank cooked an excellent batch of chili for our friends; never before had food tasted so savory. She was the head chef and Hank was the sous chef. He was clad in a green apron that read in white letters "Married, but not Dead."

Not much time passed before the Black Widow made one final appearance—she was back in town for a weekend in October, midway through the college semester. This would have been a handful of weeks into my second to last semester at university—coming to an end or coming to a new beginning. In an abomination of a home, I lived that last year. Across the street—amid the Greek life madness—was where she visited some of her old sorority friends in her final chapter of this epoch.

Lauren's friend dated Stan Green. Toward the end of the evening, a cigar wrapper was repurposed for pot smoking—a *blunt* as they were called by hip folks such as us—and was ritualistically passed around Stan and Hank's living room. With this female company and a few other acquaintances and friends, the blunt was shared. Once he kicked up his legs onto the table and crossed his arms, not much time had to pass before Hank was deeply asleep. Inadvertently, Stan's girlfriend did the same, slouching restfully onto Hank's side.

Picture a starry night, one home in the middle of a row below the twinkling sky...in a rowhome nearby, the Black Widow was with her posse of sorority girls and Hank's friend Fleary. Surely, Fleary did all he could to divert the Black Widow, but she was determined to find him. Abruptly awakening, like a helpless insect trapped in a web, he discovered the terror of the incendiary Black Widow. She freaked out at what she saw—what looked like a new romantic companionship between Hank and this unfamiliar female—an incredible final outburst, but the true end of the web of psychosis cast by the Black Widow.

* * *

My father liked to ask seemingly simple questions; but sometimes simple questions require a lot of energy to answer. It's easy to ask a simple question, such as, "Why do stories need villains?"

Are they needed for a hero to be measured—antithetically compared—as they conquer the antihero? A traditional villain causes a difficult conflict that a hero or a band of heroes must resolve. Without this conflict, there is no heroic test. To fail this test and become a disappointment, a hero may falter, perhaps due to their wavering conviction. Unearthing another identity by creating a villain this way, a villain from within.

Altogether, this string of stories may lack a villain. If

this villain-less story contained an ominous figure—one of ill intent—the cantankerous landlord of E-Courts could occupy this role. If E-Courts was a field, sometimes I felt like an inconspicuous mouse, hiding from a hawk in a tree. On the details of this man, there is no need to further expound. He was clearly a greedy son of a bitch; and anyway, I should keep his identity as vague as possible. If he knew he was the hawk in the tree, he would surely swoop down from his perch and find a way to sue me for all this book will be worth.

Hank was a plump mouse that the starved hawk could never catch. Always on the run, because he owed rent for an apartment he apparently abandoned. The arrangements of the avaricious landlord were suspicious, but his tenants were literally uncreditworthy—perhaps we were somewhat shady, as well. The landlord would stun me with his evil aura, and rapaciously demand, "Have you seen Hank Bellefonte? I know that delinquent is around here somewhere."

"No, never heard of him," I insisted.

The Black Widow was sort of a villain, too—like a pipe polluting a river, she had to be sealed shut. So he fished elsewhere, in a little stream, but ultimately, the Tarantula was just a fling. For a while, the Mother of Dragons was spoken about like she was an elusive river nymph in scholarly folklore—and Hank, the curious faun, was infatuated by this girl. Before we met at last, I heard about her many times. She was a younger biology classmate of his that had bright-blonde hair and mesmerizing blue eyes. With all due respect, she was kind of an airhead...but if you stuck with her during discourse, you would find her head was rather elated—not inflated—

and she was an excitable person. Eventually, Hank did woo the Mother of Dragons.

As a romantic partner, a creator of art, a zealous member of community, an architect of the idea of the divine, we pursue and cultivate our passions despite challenges—like darkness to light, death after life, or succumbing to depression after achieving a happy life. Like heroes and foes, are these rivaled? Does one exist in the absence of the other? Should each be conquered, or are they curated? I am probably not breaking any original ground here as a green novelist—perhaps trivializing these matters is disrespectful, too—but I figured I would take a stab at this classic theme and be frank about what I am piecemealing together.

Upon the murder of his brother and the hanging of his loving housekeeper who was wrongfully accused, Victor Frankenstein walked through the grandeur of the Chamonix Valley to Mont Blanc. Frankenstein found tranquility in nature as he escaped a complex social dilemma brought on by his malignant creation. Mary Shelley inserts her husband's poem "Mutability," so I will do the same:

> We rest—a dream has power to poison sleep.
> We rise—one wandering thought pollutes the day.
> We feel, conceive or reason, laugh or weep,
> Embrace fond woe, or cast our cares away;
> It is the same: for, be it joy or sorrow,
> The path of its departure still is free.
> Man's yesterday may ne'er be like his morrow;
> Naught may endure but Mutability![16]

The dream I told you about earlier, that really happened to me—the bright light of the divine battling against the giver of oblivion.[17] I had to tell you about the Mother of Dragons—wanted to tell you. To tell her broader story, the dream, the Black Widow—the yin before the yang—the moose chili, these all seemed like felicitous episodes.

"The landlord is looking for you," I warned.

"That guy wipes his ass with his bare hand," quipped Hank, unconcerned. Gross, I thought—not ideal. Sometimes we don't know what we want, but we are aware of what we don't want—*fish or cut bait*—shit or get off the pot. Sometimes our criteria is porcelain, vitrified, crystal clear—but sometimes you get lonely, and your criteria degrades. Aware of what we don't want—telling someone they do not possess certain negative qualities is not quite as flattering. Hold that drifting thought—like a kite flying in one of the hemispheres of your mind, wrap the string around your finger.

* * *

Gregg Allman played on the second day of the Peach Music Festival in Scranton, Pennsylvania—a few hours north of Philadelphia, an hour farther than Bear Creek Mountain. Allman was in noticeably poor physical condition and passed away a few years later; those rock musicians could really beat themselves up with the abuse of alcohol and other substances. In his autobiography, he described his descent into a heinous version of alcoholism. His older brother, Duane, lived fast and died in a motorcycle accident at the extremely young age of twenty-four. My appreciation for the Allman Brothers' music reached its height when I was about that age, or a few years younger—they were on fire when Duane was alive. I could listen to "Don't Keep Me Wonderin'" and be energized for the rest of the day. *"You were lost in a silver spoon; thought I pulled you out in time."*

After the show, we returned to our campsite and proceeded to play music until maybe four o'clock in the morning—performed unabashedly, as our neighbors were all keen to hear music. The extended weekend experience had just begun. I played acoustic guitar and was accompanied by another guitar player and three djembe players. With this ensemble, the music was highly rhythmic and felt akin to a primitive séance. Together, we marveled at the sound we were creating—circled together between trees, our spirits transcending from the mountains—or maybe we stayed put, and we invoked surrounding spirits as we played.

I was a groomsman at Smitty's wedding many years after this festival—and Wayne was the best man. Smitty was the most inspiring groom I had ever witnessed. He displayed modern masculinity to all, while directing all his love to his bride. Like my attitude regarding the intrigue of this story's lead character, Wayne's wedding speech raised a similar theme, "I won't be able to tell you how great of a guy Smitty is...would take me ten years to do that."

This twilight jam was a wonderful moment in my life. I recall Hank listening, standing with a few others—his left knee locked and leg straight, right knee bent and right leg out in front to account for the grade of the mountain. Holding a can of beer, he had a serious look on his face. As he listened to us playing, I knew he understood how we felt...felt what we felt. Though I'm trying, I likely won't be able to tell you how intriguing Hank is—but his understanding stuck out to me that evening. I could convey so little in conversation—but at that time, I truly knew I was heard. After all, a sonic, emotive interconnection was what many were seeking at those damn hippy music festivals.

* * *

So, the first night at the festival ended up being a late one, and our imbibing and dabbling led to a challenging, hungover morning. Yes, I woke up hungover and discovered Hank lying on his stomach only halfway sheltered by his tent, with his pants and underwear worn at a level that revealed about an inch or two of his ass crack—you know, maybe he was airing out his ass. The strong are getting stronger, smart are getting smarter, and the ingenious reveal ingenuity every damn day.

Sometimes, the doctor's order is good loving.[18] Gazing upon art and engaging in activities like walking through museums could be beneficial for the mind and attitude, too. You see, there are these mechanisms for happiness. The light switch can be flipped, or the flip can be switched—the proverbial match struck, and fire proliferates, and the irradiance brings an exciting sensation—power, potential, or the ability to destruct if not held with care. While burning, the fire reminds you of your mind and soul—kindled with activities like dancing to music. I hope to live a long, happy life—to be one of those limber old guys swinging around for someone to point and say, "Damn, check that old fart out!"

You know, it does not take long for a writer in rhythm to start rambling; and I, again, am rambling. So, what am

I getting at? Reel in that kite—having a sense for what you want, and what you don't want.

When Hank was with the Black Widow, he was in a dark place. With his ass hanging out the alcove of his tent, Hank was in a bit of shade, surely a brighter place than the wicked, hovering spell of the Black Widow. The Mother of Dragons walked down the slope to the festival vendors and returned minutes later with a breakfast burrito. To arouse consciousness, she held the burrito up to his nose like ammonia gas from smelling salt. Like a dog, first he smelled the burrito. In deep sleep, he was submersed in a satisfying dream—one that is so sexy, I would not be able to fully describe it. "Hank, wake up!" she patted his back.

Before he woke up from his dream, from a stranger's dream, from my dream—or maybe he woke up in heaven, or in the land of a fairy tale, "*Faun*, what the hell are you doing!?" the river nymph asked. You know how your ears hear one string of words, but another is spoken? Sometimes the words you heard were what you *wanted* to hear—the truthful ones, surprising ones, the bold words. A mondegreen—a phrase that is misheard, misconstrued—takes on a whole new meaning.

Hank awoke and rolled contentedly onto his back. He was not conjured through some evil luring of sex and drugs. He rubbed his eyes, then itched his genitalia. As her contour glimmered, the Mother of Dragons revived him—intoxicated by the scent of the burrito, polluted by the alcohol from the prior evening, he awoke to this pleasant culinary offering, and to this gorgeous young woman. The Mother of Dragons was the light that was preceded by the dark episode of the Black Widow—like a bonfire sparkling in a night sky.

I am not sure why that fire went dim, then out. They say a traveler is supposed to leave no trace as they traverse wilderness; putting out evening campfires before they go to sleep is advised. One day, I woke up and found the firepit of this chapter—ashes and charred wood. Does that sound familiar?

You know, perhaps our relationship was sort of like the life of a dog. Dogs do not live a long time, but they do live a good time. He was a good boy, that Black Floyd. Wayne had a beautiful Bernese Mountain Dog—he was a good arfin' dog, too. Ferb—the dog of my family—he was a special little puppy. When I walk alone, sometimes I picture him scuttling around by my feet; but this book isn't written to him, or for him. He was a dog, for Chrissake. No, I don't recall why the fire breathed by the Mother of Dragons went dim, then out. I suppose you and I will never know.

4

Après in Aspen

Chaz Julian was the smartest person among the group of friends, or maybe I was—I mean, look, I am writing a goddamn book. Although maybe writing a book does not require intelligence—perhaps *righteousness* is the required trait—and a writer probably needs to be *different* in some salient way: aloof, eccentric, or in a jaded condition. My sister, my confidant, recommended I aim to be profound and not pretentious.

We will see what happens as I try to market this thing—the non-writing aspect of being a writer is intimidating, like infiltrating a cult—and I don't plan on joining the Writer's Guild, give me a break. What do you think? Shall I redact this last thought if I want this book to circulate among the masses? No, it'll stay. But to serve as consolation, I could offer a quick note of gratitude to the authors of a few inspiring literary works.

Almost self-referentially, bell hooks posited that authors

are angels. She also posited that one should honor their inevitable death by enjoying life, and—at the very least—spend your days reading. To extend this first notion, if authors are like angels as she says, maybe people that recommend the book of an angel are akin to shepherds. Books, like floating clouds in a literary sky—some fly by quickly, others more slow. When you finish a thoughtful, emotionally provoking novel, there is a sadness as the sky gradually returns to blue. If by chance you are outside and the time is day, glance to the sky and search for a cloud, that's what you hold—now close your eyes. See what I mean?

So, yes, I enjoy reading. *Oliver Twist* by Charles Dickens on the train from Philadelphia to southern New Jersey. *A Farewell to Arms* by Ernest Hemingway at the diner on my lunch break. *Alexander the Great*, a biography by Philip Freeman, while I was waiting at the dentist. Like a Tao, I simultaneously balanced the profoundness within *All About Love* and *The Art of War*. At the gym, I would read between lifting sets. I would glance at the mirror-gazing, self-absorbed lunkheads, proud that a non-stop thirst for the stories and lessons within literature was what made me unlike my peers. Like the creation of Frankenstein, who read *Paradise Lost* and drew a comparison of himself and Victor to Adam and his Creator—I would be inspired by these books, as if any book was a true history.

Carl Magoin was smart, too. He received a law degree from Villanova University—earned it, was molded by it. Oh, we were all a bunch of smart dudes; but Chaz went to the University of Wyoming after we graduated from university, and I would argue he was the smartest of the bunch. Chaz studied meteorology in an area of the country where, I understand, the weather is highly unpredictable. But if anyone could predict the weather out there, God damn it, Chaz could do it...smartest son of a bitch in the group!

After Chaz earned his PhD in Meteorology, the wind blew him south to Boulder, Colorado. Chaz skied, hiked, and mountain biked. He enjoyed *craft* beer—on the cutting edge of the *craft* beer craze that started years ago, a trend that still rages as I write today—though I am starting to get burned out by all these spicy pale ales. He smoked a lot of pot and was scientific about that, too.[19] He had a girlfriend named Morgan who was tall, blonde, and attractive. Morgan was the friend—or associate—of a girl named Abby who I dated at the same time. Dating alongside Chaz and Morgan was one of the earliest romantic installments for yours truly...this occurred during sophomore year at university. On the spectrum of juvenile to mature, Chaz and Morgan teetered on the latter. Abby and I were like a couple of children with boo-boos.

Abby was my first steady girlfriend, and my housemates were not fond of her; but in those two years, not a single girl mixed smoothly into the batter. No, with each relationship I can recall, there was never a civil mingling. We all just wanted each other's undivided attention, preferred one another's unadulterated behavior, and not some charade before a partner —yes, that was probably the true apprehension.

Angelo's Mel was in a group that announced themselves as the "slam pigs." How does that sound? Not too decorous, right? She was a bit of a shameless troublemaker and put my poor friend through a lot of suffering. An aching heart, eventually broken, I guess. Abby and I would wake up in the middle of the night—for instance at 3 a.m.—to them yelling at each other. From an undeserved afternoon nap, we would wake up at 3 p.m. to them yelling at each other, too.

Years later, in Philadelphia, a few homeless people squatted behind the house where I lived for a short while. During daytime, this haggard but heart-wrenching couple would leave their camp—which was nestled in the abandoned lot directly behind our backyard fence—and return at night like nocturnal, urban critters. My housemates and I were afraid to ask these rough, down-and-out drifters to vacate.

Every evening the homeless woman led the recurring, highly audible discussion. Under the dim glow of metropolitan stars, surrounded by an overgrowth of vegetation in the vacated property, she would cackle about how they belonged with one another, and needed to survive together. She claimed that she miscarried the man's child. Some nights, I would lie in bed and wonder if that was an appropriate event to bind them together forever. On other nights, being kept awake by this riffraff was infuriating.

The photographer Corey Arnold focused on urban wildlife for a featured assignment for *National Geographic*. The first installment tracked elusive coyotes in Chicago—this work was detailed and statistical—and for the second installment, Arnold traveled to South Lake Tahoe, California. Arnold snapped an image of a massive black bear stepping through a battered wooden fence. From a den below an abandoned home, the bear emerged. How would you like that—a goddamn bear hunkered down next door?

Watching our step, with hands fastened to the finicky rail, we walked down precarious, wooden, and gapped stairs to one of the E-Courts basements. Landing on concrete ground, there we found Chaz dancing with Mel applying some stylistic backside body friction—generally acceptable in that era, but this was while she was dating Angelo. I'll tell you what—that was not a jovial situation. So Chaz Julian, and Morgan did not date forever, nor did Angelo and Mel. Over the years, Chaz and I communicated at least annually. The dating topic was usually discussed, though I don't recall if Chaz Julian dated anyone for long in Wyoming. When settled in Boulder, Colorado, he was a single man...that was the last time I checked.

Chaz and Hank were from the same hometown and had a childhood friend who matriculated at a state school of similar degree. They visited this friend and met one of his classmates, Paul "Viper" Riddo. Viper was a strange individual, and Hank got along with him instantly. They bonded over the destruction of an apartment that held a party they all attended during this visit. Discreetly, they started by dismantling the bathroom, then brought the storm outwards to other rooms in the apartment. Two kindred people from then on—now, that sounds like an appropriate incident to create an everlasting partnership.

Viper moved just southeast of the city of Boulder, to Denver, Colorado. At around the same time, a breeze brought Chaz southward. In late winter and on a whim, Hank and I joined Chaz and Viper for a wild weekend out west. Sometimes adventures—even ones that require the flight of an airplane—are best executed spontaneously.

* * *

I drove up to the Poconos maybe five times altogether

that winter and was about to declare the season over—this was just the second year I had snowboarded. At the start of the season, I bought a blank white snowboard deck and decorated the top with beer logo stickers. I acquired a robust collection at a beer festival I attended that winter in Atlantic City, New Jersey. The festival features a stripper dunk tank; what an entertaining show. Otto was an exceptional baseball player—a regular season, undefeated pitcher during our senior year at high school. On the second throw, he drilled the target. Soaked, she returned to her chair. On his third throw—again, down she fell...what a ruthless son of a bitch.

I returned a year after Millersville graduation to attend a summer beer festival, in the nearby city of Lancaster. At that time, Hank was dating the Mother of Dragons...and he finally graduated, as well. After a voracious session of drinking at the festival, we stayed at her place. Her housemate did not welcome us, or care for our drunk, satiated, and now tired state. Despite the lack of invitation, a few of us tried sleeping in their living room. Hank assured her we would cause no disruption, we would stay quietly, and would be gone early. He explained this as I lay on the floor, pretending to be asleep. I emanated a snore—partially for comedic effect—but more to help Hank convince her that our nature was harmless. Unpersuaded, she demanded we leave. So we did—and like vagrants, we slept in the graveyard next to her apartment. Who knows, maybe we're still sleeping there. With all these problems and solutions, perhaps life since then has all been an illusion.

Five trips to the Poconos would have been enough—the winter season and its snow sports were just about over when...discovering a music and ski festival in Aspen, Colorado

—informing me, "Dude, this is the deal of a lifetime"—immediately convincing me this was a journey worth taking—listing things in an odd manner to change the rhythm of this story, keeping you on your goddamn tippy toes. The purchase included two lift tickets and a few evenings of music on a stage at the base of one of the mountains. The price, roughly two hundred dollars. I was so excited I accidentally bought two tippy tickets.[20] The extra ticket I purchased was sold at a loss on the internet, but I was relieved the ticket was sold, and I then booked a ticket for an airplane from one of the budget airlines, an affordable way to get to Denver, Colorado.

On the same flight, Hank and I flew westward. At the airport in Philadelphia, we met and drank a few beers, commencing our excellent adventure; meanwhile, there were three girls flying out to the same city for their own raucous weekend. At a bar in the airport was where Hank and I first rendezvoused, and these unfamiliar girls joined us in the initial stage of our trek. Hank was able to procure one of their phone numbers—a couple of atypical Casanovas on their way to Colorado...a duo of non-traditional Don Juans. Hank as João da Ega, and I, Carlos da Maia—or perhaps the other way around...the literary figures of Eça de Queiroz, if you didn't know. To the Portuguese, this novel by Eça de Queiroz is obligatory reading.

With one of the girls, I discussed professional sports—professional basketball used to be my favorite. She was interested in being a contributor to the short-lived sports talk podcast in which I took part, *Trust the Podcast*, which was a reference to the star player's slogan "Trust the process."[21] I floated the idea of her joining the podcast by my podcast mates by sending them a picture of her—she posed for the photograph willingly, of course. Wearing a shirt with the logo of the local professional team, she looked the part; but she never appeared on the podcast. She could have been the next Taryn Hatcher! Attractive and certainly vibrant—she could have been the next Serena Winters!

After we landed and exited the plane, we bid those wild ladies a farewell and an adieu. Viper picked us up and took us to a saloon in the city of Denver. Thursday was the day of the week, and we arrived at about the time when many working people finish their work. Mitchell Swift, an exceptionally extreme mountain-trekking friend of Viper's, met us at the saloon. Spirits were high, a mile high, ehh?

Mitchell Swift joined us on our trip to Aspen—he masterminded the trip, really. His girlfriend and her friends joined us, too. The plan was to leave before sunrise the next day. Once a few beers were consumed, Viper drove us up to Boulder to sojourn at the rented home of Mitch Swift.

A long day of traveling led to an early evening. After we met his girlfriend, Ruby, out we tuckered. Hank on the sofa—I laid out on the hard, uncomfortable carpeted floor, but fell asleep in the end—satisfied vagabonds enjoying the welcome, no need of persuasion. Ruby did not give us a tough time whatsoever. Like us, Ruby was excited for the weekend to unfold.

"Are you counting sheep or going straight to sleep?" were the final words I heard that evening.

* * *

Aspen, Colorado—what do you think of when you think of this place? You think upscale, correct?

We joined a bunch of degenerates the moment we arrived. Above us were clear, blue skies, but the local air was a colorful haze of conversational nonsense, of which we too contributed with our own unique, excited emissions. In a two-bedroom condo at the Aspen Snowmass Village is where we stayed—ninety American dollars was my share for the weekend's arrangements. Couple this with the inexpensive, highly affordable travel and event fares, and the overall deal still astounds me—it was a different time, but not too long ago.

Without outright declaration, Hank set aside a few goals for the weekend. Hank wanted to shred the slopes. Alongside his friends, he sought the use of drugs and the consumption of alcohol. The man aimed to laugh, sing, dance, and engage in spontaneous comedic creation with our group and with the strangers we would meet. But Hank desired—above all—for women to reveal their bosoms.

After we settled into the condo early in the afternoon, Hank, Viper, and I split from the broader group. They had a busier ski season, and we were more excited to get out on the slopes. First, we redeemed whatever voucher information we had for a ski lift pass. Hank could be loquacious, so he took a while longer in the shop. Viper and I stood outdoors at the base village. On a bench near where we stood, a wacky girl—who appeared to have stayed awake throughout the entirety of the prior night—sat with her head in her mittens. Viper simply asked, "Are you okay?"

Like a distraught Uma Thurman playing Poison Ivy, who lost her footing and fell from the top of a tree, this girl looked upon us. With unsettling eyes, she told us about the prior evening's show at a local venue called Belly Up. She saw Umphrey's McGee, the band scheduled to play at the base of the mountain on this evening—snow or shine.

Hank exited the ticket office, joined us, and asked, "Hey, are you on drugs?" The girl confirmed—then told us about last night's rough sleeping arrangements and voiced her concern about her lack of knowledge regarding the whereabouts of any of her friends—providing bare intelligibility with all these topics, flailing her arms along the way. Absorbed, Hank listened, showing a comprehending demeanor. He then interrupted her, "Wait a second, is that 'up dog' on your chin?"

She paused and then inquired, "What's 'up dog'?"

"Not much, how about you?" Hank replied. I was in disbelief—it worked. To calm this distressed woman, he unearthed this childhood antic. On the ski lift, she then rode with us. Viper asked, "Are you sure you're good to ski?" But before she could answer...

"Can you show us your boobs? I am curious how your nipples look compared to the snow..." interjected Hank. Meeting the request, her breasts were pale, her nipples were quite pink...especially when compared to the white of the snow. Upon offloading, she parted from us—to the bar lodge at the top of the mountain, she skied. After the grand reveal, she may have been struck with a feeling of remorse. In a brief reflection on the chair in the air, she may have reinterpreted the "up dog" trick as an act of deception.

During my first run out west, I moved with caution...my guarded ride was an overall thrill, but Hank was "sending it," as they say. He hit the rollers and landed with an audible—

whisper with me—*poof!* Ahead of me, Hank and Viper would park off to the side. On the shoulder of the trail, they waited every minute or so. The pauses accomplished two things, you see—they did not lose me, for one, and they were afforded a moment to scope out exciting cliffs to jump. At the bottom of the run, Hank and Viper took celebratory doses of acid—a drug that intimidated me. I declined despite my shared feeling of triumph. I wanted all my faculties to effectively perform the sport:

f-a-c-u-l-t-i-e-s[22]

At around lunchtime, Chaz and the others merged with our little brigade. By then, Hank and I had built up an appetite. After two runs with the whole squadron, he and I decided to sit down at the mountaintop bar for a beer and burger. The girl with the pale, perky breasts was nowhere to be seen.

During the meal, Hank's eyes got wilder. Compared to my dining approach, he focused and ate his cheeseburger much more deliberately. Once the burger was completed, he was eager to go see how Viper was faring. We caught up with the team for one more run, which involved a difficult lateral traverse, much easier to do with skis. This was the first time I noticed the elevation, the first time I experienced the infamous altitudinal impact on breath.

After we agreed that we all felt thoroughly satisfied and accomplished with our mountainous exploration, we hailed a shuttle bus that took us back to the condo village. Someone pointed out that the bottom half of my face had been torched by the sun. But it was alright, the party was commencing; and soon, I would not be feeling any pain. Still, I probably looked preposterous.[23] With daylight still plentiful, we enjoyed a few beers at the condo and then relaxed at the community hot tub. After all, we were on vacation.

In this period of time, the cellphone application Snapchat reigned supreme. Now convened in the hot tub, I documented a video of Viper chugging a Coors Banquet. *And action!* He did the pour technique; the flow fell from about a foot above his mouth. He finished the can off by drenching his face and hair with the final few fluid ounces. Hank laughed. I turned and directed the camera at him—he proceeded to make monkey noises, "Hoo, hoo, hoo!" I pivoted the camera back to Viper, "Hoo, hoo!"

Hank was a very complimentary guy. Ruby's friend Ava's breasts were sort of floating at the surface—he mentioned how he thought this buoyancy was chill. "But do you think they would float better if you weren't wearing your bikini top?" She laughed, but this experiment went untested. The ensuing conversation included matters such as the blessed weather of the afternoon, and the meal we planned to eat upon our departure from the hot tub. We deliberated about our musician preferences. We discussed history, fairy tales, and much, much more.

Later, rather than running the regular shuttle buses for the trek between the condo village and the ski resorts, yellow school buses transported the hippies and ski bums to the evening festival. Climbing onboard, we took up the last few rows in the front of the bus. We arrived at the festival to find a long line that would require some patience. With levity, Hank improved the usually restless situation by telling us a lengthy joke.

Alright, I have a joke for you guys, but I gotta warn ya: this joke does not have a punchline.

Let me tell you a story about a high school friend of mine named Johnny. Johnny always waited until the last minute to do anything. Prom was like two weeks away and he still didn't have a date...but he asked out this girl he liked, and she said yes. She was a mondo babe and Johnny was stoked!

So, he went to the tuxedo shop...and he had to wait in this long line...just like this one actually. He waited in a long line with all the rest of the guys that waited until the last minute...but he didn't mind waiting because he was going to prom with a smoke show that he had been digging for a while...her name was like Gabby or something. He got his tux and then went to a flower shop. What do you call those things? Oh yeah, corsage...he went to get one of those...but what do you know...same long-ass line! I guess everybody was like waiting until the last minute to do anything. He had to pick up tickets to get into the prom...same story, long line.

Johnny's flustered the day of prom...time got away from him, and he rushed over to Gabby's after he put on his tux, and after his mom took pictures of her little Johnny.

So, Johnny and Gabby are finally on their way to prom. They're super late, like the last people there. They had to get in the very back of the line...and it took a while to get through this line because everyone was all duded up, taking pictures, "Oh my god, you look great," and moving slow. But it was all good, Johnny was going to prom with his dream babe. He didn't mind waiting in a long line.

They finally get through the door...and they're at prom...and find a really good place to stand. Gabby was thirsty and asks Johnny if he could go get her some punch. Johnny did—he walked right up to the punch bowl.

There was no punchline.

* * *

"Boots! We're looking for boots! Who's got boots?" was what we shouted as we entered the festival. We didn't realize we would be dancing in snow. I was wearing sneakers, for crying out loud. Hank too, "Anybody got boots!?" The next day we would wear our snowboard and ski footwear.

"You're *beautiful!*" the opening act sang. Along, we sang, "Your *boots* are cool!" We managed well enough, keeping our socks dry by standing in packed-down, large, snowy footprints. We discussed the "Leave No Trace" hiking and camping concept, and how one of us came across an alternative, "Leave Only Footprints." With gratitude, we concluded this situation was much better than standing in deep, printless snow.

"Leave No Trace—I wish corporate America deployed this concept in public restrooms...they can get pretty nasty," bullshitted yours truly as a gregarious man puttered up to us with an unzipped plastic bag that contained a collection of pot-infused brownies and cookies. We thanked him, accepted—I can handle that—and then onward, he started to putter. Hank shouted, testing the altruism of the stranger, "Hey wait! Do you have any boots?"

Plumes of cigarette smoke were noticeable, but not too invasive. The no-smoking policy was upheld with some courtesy. Prior to firing up a solitary cigarette, Viper and I debated the stringency of the policy. With discretion, we smoked. We understood that the idea was to prevent cigarette butts from collecting on the well-maintained ski path. "Man would ya look at all these condos, the locals are probably glaring at us with straight-up disgust! Dude just glowering!" exhaled Viper with a smile.

One year later—in the upswing of a brand-new pandemic—people of the world would find themselves confined and locked indoors. During a pandemic, one learned to cherish the comfort of home, being surrounded by an immediate clan—a pandemic suppresses wanderlust if anything. But even sans pandemic, I think this would have been the first and last Après in Aspen. The local homeowners would have found a way to put the kibosh on that ragged shindig.

* * *

The concert concluded—*It's time to get the hell out of here*. Aboard a yellow school bus loaded with satisfied concert-goers, we were taken back to the condo village. Every seat was occupied, and fun was clearly had by all seat occupiers.

What is the scientific process where there is a volume of space contained in glass surrounded by another space, each of which have different temperatures, the internal temperature being warmer than the external temperature—and then there is moisture in the internal chamber of space that collects on the cool, surrounding interior surface due to the temperature differential? Where's a goddamn meteorologist when you need one. I guess this process would be condensation, right? Condensation—imagine a shit ton of condensation on the school bus windows.

Yes, all the hippy sweat made the bus humid and warmer than the outside air temperature, so the windows on the bus were covered in condensation. The ambiance was dreamy due to these hippy catalysts in this scientific process—when I think back to that bus ride, everything's blue and silver.

Toward the back of the bus was where we sat like a bunch of cool kids—but Hank lost his cool, nudged my shoulder, "Dude, I'm pretty sure this is where we should get off."

"Nah, Hank, I know where we're going...we have a little more to go," stated Mitchell Swift calmly, looking back from the seat in front of us. At the time, I trusted him much more.

"No, this is it, look!" He wiped off some condensation that immediately re-condensated. "Ah fuck!" Hank stood up and into the aisle.

"You have to sit while the bus is in motion!" the driver shouted.

"We missed our stop!" He was really freaking out now. The rest of the bus riders were enjoying this fit of anxiety as he frantically ran up and down the aisle, "Where are we!?"

"Come on, buddy, sit *down*!" At this point, Hank was unsure whether to be panicky, wild, and genuinely concerned, or to go along with the situation, which he realized others found to be humorous.

Viper intervened, "HEY, SOMEBODY GET THIS GUY A BUS STOP!" The whole damn bus laughed hysterically—a harmonious guffaw.

* * *

The hysteria ended—*this is us, Hank, you crazy son of a bitch.* After the bus dropped us off, we ensconced ourselves at the condo for the remainder of the evening. In the living room space, we smoked and drank. Ruby's friend—who hailed from Wyoming—seemed like the leader. She dimmed the lights, chose the music, and gathered her girlfriends in the open space. To her band of vixens, she then distributed hula hoops and brandished a similar device herself. For spectating, Chaz, Mitch, Hank, and I found seats on the couch. Together, they became a galactic swirl of light, at which to simply marvel. Awestruck, Hank muttered to me, "Dude, I like this."

With each hula hoop rotation, their bodies were outlined. A sparkling, whip-looking object would latch on, trace, and release from the contour of the lead woman's swirling frame like itinerant star dust in outer space. Quietly, I responded, "Hank, me too."

With his arms crossed, Viper was asleep on a stool. But Chaz, Mitch, Hank, and I were mesmerized by this group of friends—above the nebula, the leader looked in our direction with a ravishing, entrancing facial expression—it was like she was synchronizing some futuristic mating dance. Hank could not contain himself anymore, announcing to all, "I had *no* idea women from Wyoming were like this—"

* * *

Dust of evening settled; the séance was complete. Now the morning dew glistened as droplets of little secrets. We awoke and drove northward, to the main highway which would bring us back to the city of Denver. At Carbondale, on the way to this main road, we stopped and swam in hot springs. The men of our brigade wore shorts or underwear. With the bathing suits they packed, the women anticipated the stop. Sun shining, cloudless, bluebird skies, mountains in the distance above the Roaring Fork River—we floated, enjoying the warmth of the shallow hot springs and the views of sharp mountain peaks.

"Man, this place is beautiful," I avowed.

"Yeah dude, this is *definitely* where I parked my car," agreed Viper.

"Ava, your breasts would look *great* with the mountains in the background ...do you think I could take a picture of them!?" with a grin, Hank inquired. Trust somehow earned—or perhaps gained through some sort of process, if you will—she finally agreed to his request. Smiling for the camera, she crossed her arms and lifted her shirt over her head, over her wild red hair. Ava's breasts were rather large. In the foreground of the image, they gallantly shined. Like a modern, American goddess, Ava stood tall. Behind her rose the crests of the Rocky Mountains, above that the bluest skies imaginable. Yes, Hank was an imaginative photographer—you know, he had an artistic eye.

5

Photographic Memory

The first time I viewed a nude body part on the big screen...do you really want to know? Ben Stiller's zipper-jammed testicle in the movie *There's Something About Mary* is the answer. Phew, that looked painful.

On a winter morning, Hank picked me up at a parking lot outside of Philadelphia. His truck was filled to the roof with shit. Deer antlers hung from his rearview mirror and clanked against the windshield when potholes were hit. Hank would whisper, "Easy there, fella."

On a miniature chair glued to the dashboard, a stuffed moose sat, smiled, and waved. "Where'd you get that thing?" I asked.

"One man's treasure was once another man's trash..." I gazed at an apple core in the center console and wondered where it resided on this spectrum. We drove up to Blue Mountain in the Poconos for a day trip of snowboarding. He took a sip of coffee, then returned the cup to the holder—flipped the sun visor down and said, "Dude, check this out," while reaching for a photograph clipped to the visor's underside—an original photograph of a girl holding her exposed, voluptuous breasts. Picturesque tatas...I'm telling you; the man had a gift—an artistic eye.

Hank had a younger brother who was gay, and this amateur model was a friend of his—imagine the classic platonic friendship between a gay male and a straight woman, where there was a sense of safety, a peacefulness that was not obfuscated with any sexual tension; perhaps that is enough to describe the dynamic between the three of them. Hank spoke highly of his brother, and I don't think he malevolently breached their space, which was meant to be mutually free of any wooing. I just found that to be curious, right? This story of companionship between a gay man and a heterosexual woman—in a world of underlying sexual tension across the sexes—and in came Hank, the macho older brother, to pop the asexual bubble.

On the brink of popping was Stiller's zipper-jammed testicle—would have been one hell of an explosion for that first televised display of nudity. As time passes, photographs and videos become more than a pastiche of the past. They are reference points for our otherwise fading memories. The earliest memory I maintain—unaided by photograph—took place at Nussex Farms. I was a toddler, and my sister was a goddamn baby.

Like diminutive, colorful cotton balls in our puffy winter gear, we were pulled through the snow on a mint-green sled by our father. With snow falling heavily and already accumulated on the ground—deep and lumpy—the three of us trekked through the apple orchard near our home. My sister was behind me as I sat dutifully at the bow. Along the ride, I suddenly sensed her paltry presence was gone. She must have fallen off the sled! Grabbing hold of one of the sled edges, twisting my toddler body around, I looked back through the thick snow to find the vague hue of my helpless sister about twenty feet away, floundering in the snow—cried to my dad to stop so we could rescue the poor baby. Dawdling, fading into the wonderland of snow-covered apple trees, this image is frozen in my mind.

Regarding the photographed boobs, "Woah they're nice!" commented yours truly. He agreed, "Dude, she's got some mondo jugs!" He then wedged the photograph back in the clip, took another coffee sip, and we proceeded with our trip. Ehh?

* * *

Upon exiting the northbound highway that leads to Blue Mountain, one finds a valley containing grassy knolls, naturally architecting a landscape unlike the rolling and wooded terrain typical of Pennsylvania. Here, we discussed the need for an internet forum that ranked the best live versions of Grateful Dead songs. Via vote from the fanbase, a list could be compiled. "Dude, I hate when you go to show someone a Grateful Dead song and you pick a real stinker!" We were listening to a flat version of "Me and My Uncle."

Hank descended the mountain at an impressive speed. "If I was a Native American, they'd call me Chief Haulin' Ass," was how he responded to a compliment. While on the mountain, we met his friend—the ex-girlfriend of a "boating buddy." She too kayaked, and kayaking was the only subject that they were bent on discussing. At lunch, I was rendered mute. Belligerently, I eventually asked, "Do you guys talk about skiing when you kayak?" Hank again silenced me, "No, dude, we talk about kayaking!"

After a brief pause, "You guys really like kayaking that much, huh?"

"I've tried my hand at the Bible, tried my hand at prayer, but nothing but water brings my soul to bear." She affirmed her obsession, too. I was unsure as to who he was quoting, but I recalled J.R.R. Tolkien's description:

> *Ulmo is the Lord of Waters. He is alone. He dwells nowhere long but moves as he will in all the deep waters about the Earth or under the Earth. He is next in might to Manwë, and before Valinor was made he was closest to him in friendship; but thereafter he went seldom to the counsels of the Valar, unless great matters were in debate. For he kept all Arda in thought, and he has no need of any resting place. Moreover, he does not like to walk upon land, and will seldom clothe himself in a body after the manner of his peers. If the Children of the Eru beheld him they were filled with a great dread; for the arising of the King of the Sea was terrible, as a mounting wave that strides to the land, with dark helm foam-crested and raiment of mail shimmering from silver down into shadows of green. The trumpets of Manwë*

are loud, but Ulmo's voice is deep of the deeps of the ocean which he only has seen.[24]

Some of his shirts contained simple portraits of a fish, bear, or cat—others were intricate, tribal patterned shirts printed on what seemed to be sturdy fabric, his raiment surely unbranded—but he would have likely preferred the *Ulmo* approach—unclad, no clothing at all.

At around this time, Hank became more and more seafaring. If anyone deserved the moniker Lord of Waters, that personage was Hank; and likewise, if anyone earned the right to be revered as Lord of Flies, well, you know, the worthy recipient would be The Master.[25] On commercial fishing fleets launching from all along the Eastern Seaboard, Hank examined chemical levels of fish to be sacrificially converted to seafood for the hungry masses. He did this work as an agent of the federal government. Due to opposing views of later government mandates, he then transitioned to strenuous work on these fleets as a deckhand, mostly harvesting the deep sea for scallops. For weeks at a time, gone fishing on the deep blue sea.

Paul Salopek is a contemporary explorer. As a commercial fisherman, he began his career. Before Hank and I were born, he joined a fleet out of New Bedford, Massachusetts. Before that, Salopek studied biology—just like Hank. His fishing assignments were sporadic, and he worked as a journalist as well. Eventually, he became a featured writer in *National Geographic*. Salopek was one of my favorite *National Geographic* writers—a Pulitzer Prize winner who documented a fascinating walk, in a project called *Out of Eden*—the *Camino* he undertook replicated the early dispersal of humanity. With a lot of work ahead of us, I prefer to believe that Hank is gravitating to something special, maybe similar to the eventual career of Salopek—a slow journalist who demonstrated patience as he observed a range of humanity and our anthropogenic effects on the planet as time unfolded.

As the words of this book are brought into existence—letter by letter from fingers tapping a keyboard at the same old desk, for Chrissake—he takes new steps, each preceded by a decade more of steps. He embarked on the *Out of Eden* walk when I graduated from university—first set out from the Horn of Africa.

As a commercial fisherman, Hank would depart from ports up and down the Atlantic Coast—a real, modern mariner—but sometimes his fishing was more recreational in nature. Those were the trips that I got excited about...

* * *

As I peacefully strolled along the cliff walk in Newport, Rhode Island, I looked out to sea—maybe Hank was out there somewhere past the foggy veil that surrounded the coast—and I arranged some passages for this book on the chalkboard of my quixotic mind. If this were a movie with music, "Lucky Man" by The Verve would be audible. I decided that this slice of reflection could start here—and in the next chapter, or maybe the chapter after that, I can tell you what I was doing in Newport—non-linearity worked for Quentin Tarantino, maybe that style will be effective in this modest collection of stories.

Early in the morning, I parked on Narragansett Avenue

and strolled along the cliff walk. In Newport, I rambled later that day, and camped nearby on Jamestown Island at night. The trip ended the next afternoon at a restaurant called the Red Parrot on Thames Street. Two light beers were drunk at the Red Parrot, and the New England Clam Chowder was pretty tasty—but the tuna I ate as the main serving was the *second* best serving of tuna I had ever eaten—which is saying a lot, let me tell you.

Years before, I was sitting on the beach. I faced southward, the sun approaching the land-based horizon to my right, when I received a call from Hank. I answered, "Talk to me."

"No, you first," he responded, refusing to be disoriented by that usual initial answer he had heard before...

I laughed and replied, "Nicely done."

"Dude, are you in Ocean City?" he asked with excitement, wind whipping in the background.

"Sure am. Beautiful day here!"

"Sick! I'll be getting into Sea Isle in like an hour, ya damn land lubber. I'm out fishing with my buddy—I caught some *fat* tunas!"

He arrived later that night while my family and neighbors were all collected in the alley behind our houses. We were in the midst of a party, beach chairs arranged in a circle on the stone driveways. After introductions and some snacking, we began cooking in the garage. Some of the fish was eaten raw, and we pan seared the rest on a portable electric grill—Hank wielding the spatula, "Did I ever tell you my bacon story?"

"Nope, let's hear it," I said without hesitation.

"Alright, so I was with the Mother of Dragons at the time...was a hot morning in the summer, we both woke up at her apartment. This was after an evening where we were at a concert, drinking all night, I think the show was in Harrisburg...and when we got back we shagged for hours. So, the next morning we needed sustenance...I mean I was depleted in many ways.

"She made us Bloody Marys and she was sitting at the kitchen counter while I had the bacon cooking, dicing up the potatoes...was going to use the grease from the bacon to make home fries. Her kitchen started getting hot, so I took off my shirt while I was splitting up the spuds."

With spatula in hand, now raised for effect, "I went over to the stove and grabbed the spatula to swish the bacon...then POP! The bacon grease exploded from the pan and splattered right between my nipples." He pointed to the spot with the spatula, then moved the kitchen device slowly downward. "The grease quickly streamed down my stomach and collected like a pool in my fuckin' belly button. I screamed the whole way down, 'AHHH!'"

"Damn!" I laughed. My sister was wide-eyed, appalled.

"I know, dude. I'm an apron man now...the grease left a physical burn mark for months...but the mental burn mark will last for fuckin' eternity."

"That sure sounds traumatizing," my sister sympathized.

In the garage—surrounded by chairs, umbrellas, and other beach items—we stood and ate the fish. Soy sauce was all the additional flavor that was wanted. That night, he served us the *best* tuna. My sister and I always agree.

"That's some damn good fish...you want another beer?"

* * *

In a memoirist state of tranquility, I brainstormed and walked along the cliffs with happiness coming and going. I passed the breakers, the mansions, and castles, walked along to the terminus at Bailey Beach. Turned around, headed up Bellevue Avenue back to where I parked my car at the start of the walk. The time was still relatively early when I returned to my car at Narragansett Avenue—all along the way, I thought about what I wanted this book to accomplish.

Writing a memoir is walking alone on train tracks in the woods, curves in the distance to tracks beyond, out of sight. Waiting for someone to appear from the bend, imagining their emergence—to encounter some stranger, to encounter your future, realized self, but he never appears. Life, a deer, and a stream running, robins and cardinals flying; death, a downed tree, and a crushed can of beer discarded. Reading a book, like pondering graffiti on a boulder. You could probably walk the tracks to a memoir, too. At the very least, we should all be dilettantes.

But I am telling the tale of Hank Bellefonte, and I'm not embellishing a goddamn thing. He is the most interesting person I will likely ever come to know, and to know him like I do makes me proud. Concerning this writing affair, he might be my edge to stardom. To be read, the dream in the distance. And when we get closer to the end of this book, I will tell you why I was able to finish—that is, the motivation will be clearer because it is an abnormal feat, writing a book. Writing what is ultimately a memoir in your late twenties and early thirties is pretty damn weird too, right? But as I strolled through Newport, Rhode Island, the overarching purpose of the endeavor was taking form. Shorter insertions—like this upcoming one—materialized as well.

After a somewhat heinous car accident in my mid-twenties, I became a "yes-man" like Jim Carrey in *Yes Man*—a tolerable movie with a relatable theme. In 1994, Carrey quickly became king, on top of the world of Hollywood in my opinion. *Ace Ventura: Pet Detective*—*The Mask*—*Dumb and Dumber*...what a prolific year of acting. Though I understand *Ace Ventura: Pet Detective* did not age well—the apathetic ending jests at the transgender community. "Einhorn's a man!"

Five guys in the car, including the driver—I was one of three in the back, stuck in the middle. We all had our legs bunched up because a folding table was running in front of us across the backseat. Through an intersection, we proceeded forward, and we collided with another vehicle, T-boned as they say. Upon impact, the car we were in immediately moved leftward, rammed by a massive SUV, perhaps a Cadillac Escalade. I wondered if that table was reinforcing at all, collecting the force of the impact—Ford was the vehicle we drove, and Fords are "built Ford tough." Smitty sat to my right—he was a tough dude, too. Five and twenty years of age. Duane Allman was twenty-four when he passed—each day is a gift for us all...like we hid our own Easter eggs. I love those sons of bitches. We were stupid and lucky, and now life is our fortune.

Like a "yes-man," I wanted to focus on my intellect and absorb knowledge in a formal setting after the car accident, or "undertake a voyage of discovery to the land of knowledge," as stated by Victor Frankenstein's friend Clerval.[26] So I applied to graduate school. I also wanted to be a yes-man when it came to invitations, especially invitations to live music events.

This upcoming sub-chapter portrays the vanished incidents that would have proceeded an invitation that I denied despite being a self-proclaimed yes-man. As I walked along the cliffs in Newport, I thought about how I could complement this book by briefly noting an event of which I did not partake.

Much of this work relies on actual occurrences—deploying imagination is more difficult. But my discernment is unique, and when one's prior perceptions are recounted like so, well, I'd argue it's not all that different from imagination. Who are all these people? Can you tell? And whether these stories are altogether bombastic or truly worthy of note, well again, you can be the judge. I embarked on a voyage the day after that car accident, a voyage of discovery to the land of knowledge, to the land of thrill—but I declined one invitation: "Dude, floating down the Colorado River for two weeks is out of my league."

* * *

Let these fictitious people begin with a sneeze that echoed once off the canyon wall to the north, and here reverberations of this incredible respiratory trumpet blast come again. "You alright, man?" she asked.

"No, somebody bless me, for the love of God," he responded, then figured the dust made him sneeze.

"Four hundred million years' worth of it, ehh?" She then let her mind imagine a reversal of the many ages of erosion, snow melt after snow melt until the Grand Canyon was a flat plain in the infancy of Earth; or, maybe the terrain of Laramidia on the other side of the Western Interior Seaway was more hilly or mountainous? She envisioned a flat plain connecting the north rim to the south rim of the canyon.[27] Entering the Colorado River, floating through the great carve out of the west like a gang about to start up their land speeders on Tatooine in *Star Wars*. From the north, they entered the canyon—might as well have floated to the Gulf of California and beyond...

Across the country, a caravan of kayakers drove. From east to west, 2,500 miles of road chasing and racing the sun a few times. Six thousand feet of arid-land erosion carved in the deepest section of the Grand Canyon, but their kayaker caravan was offered a more accessible route to the river by members of a tribe of Native Americans near Lee's Ferry in Arizona.

Along the drive out to the southwest, they sojourned in Colorado for a briefer kayaking experience. Carrying his boat down a steep grade to a rapidly flowing river, Hank lost his footing and pulverized his tailbone on a damn rock. Due to the mist from the rapids, the step was slick and the traction from his boot was no match. So, for the duration of their stopover in Colorado, Hank rested. Broken, his ass might have been.

At the entrance point near Lee's Ferry, they met the other men and women of their party; each of them brought a boat. Additionally, a round raft stored much of the provisions, and served as a stable, floating base for the explorers. Like insects in a great groove of paved sidewalk after rain, they slowly drifted down the section called the Redwall Cavern.

Deposited, they slept on beaches under walls like they were held by massive hands with fingerprints indicating epochs.

After the first rapids, they came to Nankoweap Granaries with vegetation along beaches of silt making up the fork between the Colorado River and Nankoweap Creek. Here, setting up camp again, barren slopes above. Despite the pain in his rear end, Hank persevered each day. On the trip, he broke three chairs. He had to support his weight on feeble arm rests...his ass couldn't handle the load on its own.

And on an epic excursion such as this, there has to be at least one coward, an anxious individual questioning every decision. About scorpions, he was most concerned. Whenever they began to set up camp, he would raise awareness about scorpions—made his worry everyone's top priority.[28]

Another person in the group was the early riser. Every morning he would clean up the camp, make breakfast, and brew coffee for the crew. Hank woke to the aroma of coffee, the sound of crushed beer cans, the site of a rising sun high above each blessed day. Still, the pain in his ass was almost unbearable.

But by the sixth day, it was the coward that became unbearable. Hank argued a scorpion sting was like the sting of a bee—if one had a calm head on their shoulders, they could view a scorpion sting as a psychedelic experience, for Chrissake. So, after setting up camp on the sixth evening, a few of them harvested scorpions, and they administered scorpion doses to one another. On the tush, Hank let the scorpion sting away...his ass went utterly numb. On that trip, the sixth evening was Hank's best night of sleep. Under the stars, this sedated snooze was supreme.

But on the seventh morning, Hank woke to a sun well past the horizon of the canyon rim. The air he smelled was dusty but clean, free of pollution, with no trace of French roasted and pressed coffee. Scurrying animals and a rolling river were the noises he sensed. In a panic, he examined the early riser—unzipped his tent to discover a twitching man with eyes moving rapidly, uncontrolled. Serious symptoms were unlikely, Hank argued...but they tested the odds with five people, and one was dealt a crappy hand.

Rather than elaborating on severe bodily convulsions and dire opinions, I'll just say that—miraculously—the early riser's health quickly improved. For those forty-eight hours of extreme illness, Hank felt guilty and very concerned; but upon the early riser's return to wellbeing, spirits also rose for those final days of the excursion.

Shadows were cast on the right bank in the mornings, and to the left bank in the afternoons as the kayakers marveled the metamorphic layers of the canyon. Hikers marveled at the aquatic travelers on trails imprinted above, casting shadows of their own upon the river. Footprints vanished to the wind, paddled ripples mixed up in rapids downstream—shadows cast by the walls of the canyon, by the brave adventurers, bravery of countless degree. By the third broken chair and on the eleventh day, they had reached their destination.

Here, I tap letters on a keyboard, like a pool of water glistening in the sun, magically cast on a screen above like the wall of a small canyon to the west—and I, the canyon wall of the east, in the morning with the sun on the back of my head. Undiscovered, a beautiful canyon lies before me. A much different adventure, I am on—and who knows where this adventure will take me—to the Gulf of California, to a delta of discovery? Do you think this adventure will take me anywhere at all? Will this unwavering memoirist survive the rapids, enjoy the peace of the slower portions of the river, stay warm during the storms of night...like Hank and his Merry Hanksters.[29]

"Four hundred million years, you know what I was just thinking?" he began.

* * *

To the southwest, my father and I traveled. As we age, scenes from each of these special trips blend together like an unframed collage, cherished in our minds. A mosaic of memories, carried with us like charred wood serving as coals to the fire of our lineal kinship—I believe this is a fire that my father tends as well, stoked by starting with three simple words, *do you remember...*

When we are not exercising our memory like this, these experiences manifest as we undertake new projects, together in motion and aimed forward. With no knowledge, we took up sailing. My father, the captain of the catamaran—and I, the first mate. A couple of shitty sailors, but a determined crew, we would figure out how to sail. Learn the lingo, strengthen our agility to better provide ballast on the catamaran trampoline, like dancing a tango as we tacked. I was the jib-man—the front sail I'd handle with nimbleness. My heavier father, slow at the stern, controlled the rudders and the blocks for the main sail.

We inherited no intelligence and received an odd mixture of help and discouragement from the seasoned sailors that also stored their sailboats at the beach where our vessel was kept. When he was a child, my father went sailing with his dad. My grandfather could not resolve being "in irons" and they had to get towed back to where they rented the boat.

Unadvisedly, my dad and I ran with the wind. We capsized and were thankfully dragged to shore by the breaking waves, the boat defeated on its side, the mast and sail submerged. Wheeling the boat back to its spot on the beach was a shameful duty, and arduous, too. We returned to find a concerned collection of the seasoned sailors who were minutes away from calling the coast guard.

Drank beers on the deck later that evening, discussing the danger of the sport and how maybe they were right. We didn't know what the hell we were doing. We should have considered taking steps back, maybe get lessons, refrain from sailing altogether until we were better trained; shit, maybe we should even sell the fuckin' thing. Evil can be spread in word like malicious gospel, the beach captain's strong words left us feeling morose, defeated like the image of our capsized boat getting beaten to shore.

Drank coffee on the deck the following morning, continuing the conversation, neither of us offering any fragment of optimistic outlook, until my mother slid open the door, "Check this out!" A large sailboat was on the television, anchored a few blocks away from our beach home—ran aground, was getting rocked by sizable waves. With the boat in the background—a dramatic scene—the interviewed captain looked like an old salt. To the reporter, he told his tale as he waited for a tugboat to arrive to help him dislodge his boat from shore.

The news report was like a sign from God…or a simpler, less theological message like "Hey, shit happens." That was enough sailing for this summer—but we held onto the boat and were resolved that the next summer would be more smooth sailing.

Between my junior and senior years when I was at university—one and twenty years was my age—that was when my father and I first embarked on a southwestern expedition. On our first trip, my pop and I stayed at hotels as we crossed the country like a couple of modern frontiersmen. We did not camp—the first time I slept in a tent was a few years after that—but on the second trip to the southwest, we slept in a tent I purchased for a music festival. I've still got that trusty ole tent, red and white with grey duct tape on broken seams. Can you picture that tent?

These first two trips to the southwest were well-planned excursions. First, my mother dropped us off at a train station in southeastern Pennsylvania. She whispered the customary "watch your father" send-off while she hugged me before we stepped on the train.[30] In five hours, we arrived in Pittsburgh—then the second train brought us to Chicago. We stayed in Chicago for a few nights, shared a bucket of beer at an authentic blues bar called Kingston Mines. After a day of walking around the city, a bucket of cold beers sure tasted great. The Magnificent Mile was walked, and a handful more.

We then rode on a sleeper train to Albuquerque, New Mexico—before boarding, we bought a bottle of whiskey and mixed the liquor with ginger ale. Escorted to the diner car, we wobbled as we walked, half from the locomotive inertia, half from the buzz brought on by alcohol. The meals on the train were surprisingly delicious. In the diner car, we crossed the Mississippi River and ate our meal with a train-riding enthusiast—he had a blog focused on this theme. I didn't consider him strange at all. It was a mystical ride on the *Southwest Chief*—and someday, I would also at least like to ride on the *California Zephyr*. I hope my pop will join me.

On the first trip to the southwest, we zigzagged our way to Phoenix, Arizona via rental car—and on the second, our zigzagging ended in Las Vegas, Nevada. Like a tacking sailboat, I draw a route with my pointer finger on the table for effect—it's an intriguing journey that romantic prospects seemed to enjoy. In a new professional setting, I was with a group of people that chatted through icebreaker questions. *If you could go back to any moment in your life, what would that moment be?* With a sappy tone, I described the first twenty-six-hour train ride to Albuquerque with my father. I had to leave the goddamn room to collect myself. Some icebreaker question...

My dad's a strong man; and at the time, he had a large stomach that he did not hide. Jokingly, my family called him "fat boy." In Chicago, I'd board the train with the fat boy if I could return to any moment. I'd like to retire in the southwest—perhaps in Flagstaff, Arizona. I could open a diner. I enjoy cooking breakfast while listening to music—maybe the Mrs. will work the cash register, collect some of the orders, and read out loud to the cook and our patrons. We'd call the place Fat Boy's Diner.

These experiences helped me devise a similar trip to the Grand Canyon with my good friend Otto. On the South Rim of the Grand Canyon, at Mather Campground, Otto and I stayed. In eight hours, we trudged down the South Kaibab

Trail, ascended the Bright Angel Trail, and plodded our final steps to a bar at one of the lodges—the so-called rim-to-river-to-rim route. We were beasts—more than ordinary men. Upon our first celebratory sip of beer, we joined an elite contingent of people. Even the damn mules would say we were nuts. Later in life, I met a person who worked for a few years down in the canyon, at the Phantom Ranch Lodge. I told this authority about our trek—he was genuinely impressed by the short time it took.

You see, my father imparted the wisdom required to forge and lead solo adventures of my own—to the west and beyond, no longer imaginary...rather the distant and unknown was a place in itself to bravely discover. Discover it, capture this new image with a camera...or create a memory to slowly fade away.[31] In a journal, one can write. I suppose this book is like a shared journal. One's experiences can be recorded just like this...and if they're not, will they become stories within books at a forgotten library?

With some things that are forgotten, there's hope they will be remembered, honored. Writing a memoir like this is wielding a camera, exploring your past. I could wield a paintbrush, and everyone would come to look. As a writer, I've chosen to make my life and my mind an open book.

6

A Commune in Vermont

In the mighty state of Connecticut, I became a resident of the city of New Haven.[32] So now Hank and I were both New Englanders. In New Haven, I found comfort and met a core group of friends within months of arrival, at a party on Halloween. I did not expect the grass to be so green in New Haven; sometimes the grass doesn't have to be greener...just needs to be a different shade.

New Haven is a coastal city situated on the Long Island Sound. About an hour past New York City, it's sort of the gateway to New England. East Rock—where I lived in the small city—was a neighborhood next to a four-hundred-foot geological feature of the same name. On many mornings, I sat on a rocking chair with coffee in hand. From the deck of my second-story apartment, I could see the leafage atop the red rockface. East Rock also bordered the campus of Yale University. Rocking forward in the morning, graduate students like a school of fish, like the tide of an ocean, went from right to left. Rocking back in the afternoon, they all headed left to right.

Gjoa Haven is a stop along the route of the Northwest Passage. Gjoa means *beautiful* and was the name of the first vessel to successfully complete the fabled sea route. In the summer of 2022, *National Geographic* explorer Mark Syncott and his team completed the voyage in a forty-seven-foot sailboat that starts west of Greenland at the Davis Strait and terminates in Alaska. Docking at Gjoa Haven must be a real relief. This stop is near where the British exploring expedition led by Sir John Franklin went missing in the middle of the nineteenth century. In the early twenty-first, his ships were found.

Maybe New Haven was a haven years ago, a harbor providing shelter for boats landing from God-knows-where. Prior to colonization, an area inhabited by Native Americans; left Africa tens of thousands of years ago, migrated through Asia, then moved like an hour hand across the upper half of the Pacific Rim to the Americas, taking some circuitous eastward route to find this haven in heaven—pristine land untarnished by man. After some unequitable deal with the Quinnipiac tribe, New Haven—urbanized over time—became a small city on the Long Island Sound. T.S. Lewis imagined Prince Caspian, an orphan to betrayed and murdered parents. Young Prince Caspian wondered who was conquered in Narnia.

To find a beach worth sitting on along the Long Island Sound, I had to drive eastward for about five and twenty minutes. I was a bit disappointed by this—I was hoping New Haven would contain a satisfactory recreational coastline. Despite this lack of coastline, the architecture in my neighborhood had a coastal trace...combined with a Victorian tinge to which I was not accustomed. East Rock—the homes and the people—made for a charming neighborhood. I lived on the second story of a three-story flat with two units on each floor. The façade of the building faced north, the left side of the building to the east. In the morning—and if the clouds weren't too thick—the sun would shine through my windows.

Separating my flat from the one next door was a thin wall, a lovely couple on the other side. First, I met the female. From the Newport Folk Festival, she had just returned. With an afternoon cup of coffee, this new friend met me on the deck. Her partner was a carpenter who returned to his hometown after time spent in California. His grandmother had recently passed away and he inherited her bungalow on the sound. They were adventurous, too. They backpacked in the White Mountains of New Hampshire. Up to Maine they drove, followed bands down the coastline for the weekend.

We all liked the same music, attended a few shows together. Through the thin wall, I could hear the tunes they played. And when they called to one another from across the room, they'd use the word "babe." With this couple, I got along very well. When they moved to Lake Tahoe, the music through the wall ceased...like the needle on a record player made it to the middle.

New York City—in the middle, between my home and the farther away, northeastern part of the country—had been a barricade that made New England virtually inaccessible all my life; getting to the big city felt like a big logistical deal to begin with...and now that I was living on the other side of this roadblock, the whole region seemed in reach. Could crash anywhere, a commune in Vermont...for example.

* * *

What is a commune? A collection of people, families, or individuals who live together, work together with certain responsibilities, and share common space and possessions. How does that sound? With labor and a resource development plan, a dynamic commune is a small economy that could be bartered or dictated. If you strip out that interaction, I suppose the same space could simply be characterized as a multi-family, or multi-unit, home; perhaps that is a more appropriate description of Hank's living arrangements at this time.

If Jim Carrey was king in the mid-nineties of the twentieth century, the torch was passed to Leonardo DiCaprio in the late nineties and was held by him into the 2000s. *Titanic*, young love never depicted better in any other film.[33] As for *The Beach*, I mean I thought that movie was acceptable—one of those situations where the novel was much better than the film. When Hank told me where he lived, I pictured *The Beach* and the backpacker community that DiCaprio's character daringly discovers in Thailand.

The movie captures the era effectively, documenting the advent of internet and telecommunication technologies that spurred the adventurousness of the generation. Traveling abroad had expanded possibilities then, each trip beginning with free information shared on the internet—like a commune in the ether. DiCaprio sitting behind one of those bulky, turquoise computers—cutting edge at the time—funny stuff, a cinematic blast from the past. Did you read *The Beach*? I can't picture that book on your stacked shelf.

"Get your ass up to Vermont and crash at my place," was his offer. There was a snowstorm in the middle of the week, and he was delivering me updates, "Dude, the powder was unreal today...more coming tomorrow." Like DiCaprio mapping out his international excursion, I had my eyes fixed on the weather in northern New England, the trail statuses at the mountain resorts. Finally, I woke up early on Saturday, brewed myself some coffee, and drove north. In the Mad River Valley, I met him at the Arbol de Azucar Mountain Resort.

He was working part-time at the mountain, set me up with a discounted lift ticket as a perk of the job, and his boss was Mr. McGee. Factoring in the hospitality and the discounted lift ticket, I told him several times I would pick up the tab at Lawson's after we wrapped up our shred session. That's right, a couple of chicken senders that day.

He was able to get a few runs in with me before the confinement of his labor, and a few more during his shift. His gear was in an employee locker room, and we walked there first. With my board implanted in a pile of snow near the building, we entered and were greeted by Mr. McGee. Upon the expansive mountain map painted across the wall, we looked. In a parlance I half understood, they discussed a mysterious pass through the glades between runs—referencing the twenty-foot-wide map, Mr. McGee pointed with a ski pole—this would be our first destination.

* * *

Hank carried his weight well as a skier. He sped off after we emerged from the glades—though close enough, I could hear him singing, *"Take it, to the limit!"* He leaned with all his might into every turn...*take it, to the limit!* Not shying away from bumps and airing all rollers that would send him soaring—hold on, slow down there, will ya? Sing with me, *you gotta take it* [pause] *to the limit* with style and grace that can only be achieved through absolute bravery. *You better take it* [pause] *to the limit* hitting a ramp, blasting off, and flying in the air for what seemed like ten seconds, perhaps one hundred feet in the distance—stomping the landing, maintaining speed, *one more time!*

At around three in the afternoon, I decidedly finished, that was plenty of shreds for one day. Hank had to work a few more hours. To pass the time, I read *All Quiet on the Western Front* at the lodge. I then became weary and used my jacket as a pillow while resting my eyes on a secluded bench. When I snapped out of my rest, I drove northward with Mount Ellen to my left, accompanied by a high setting sun behind thick clouds; drove toward Lawson's Brewery. I convinced myself that I saw Hank getting one final send in for the day—on the most savory trail—to stifle his longing for thrill which would otherwise strike him at some point during the boredom of night. All alone at the end of the evening, with the bright lights faded to blue.

Alexander the Great did not like to sleep either because sleep made him feel mortal...sex too, for that same reason apparently. Alexander the Great restrained from both with only occasional romps and snoozes. "Love empowers us to live fully and die well"—another lesson of bell hooks—and Hank loved wringing the day's towel dry, getting every drip from it in the pursuit of thrill. He sought this feeling of excitement hell-for-leather in a devoted, appreciative manner.

Once I arrived at Lawson's, I checked with the hostess to see if I could leave my car in the parking lot overnight, then Hank and I could consolidate to one vehicle as the rest of the unplanned evening unfolded. I also figured his place was set back in the woods through winding, partially plowed roadways. I sat at a table with a glass of beer still filled to the top—held my book open with my left hand, thumb on the left page and pinky on the right, and then took a sip, raising the glass with my other hand—ehh, might as well take another one. I peered around the bar room. The place was packed with elated skiers and snowboarders wearing wintry garb. Wait, that was pretty damn tasty. I licked the foam off of my mustache.

Dove back into the trenches with Paul Bäumer but could only read a few pages—read through the dramatic scene where Bäumer killed a man in hand-to-hand combat and was forced to watch him slowly die. Hiding alone in a bloody, muddy pit on the front that never budged. In solitude, I sat and finished a beer. On the table, I left my book, walked to the bar, and got another beer—back at the table, I opened and quickly closed the book—too much misery for this cheerful place.

Returning to the world above my book, I scanned the bar and looked at the hostess. Her eyes were following the figure of a new patron who she greeted upon entrance—there he was. "Yo, Hanky boy, over here!" waved yours truly. Like a war comrade, his right hand firmly grabbed my right forearm, and I did the same—left hand then gripped the right shoulder. We nodded our heads in an unspoken and orderly fashion, and then we separated. He looked at the table, "What are you, some sort of half-assed librarian with that thing?"

I laughed. "Nice—did I tell you about the time I called a girl a 'half-assed engineer'?"

"Hold on, let me get a beer—what are you drinking?"

"Sip of Sunshine—"

"Dude, you gotta get Little Sips!" Already in motion toward the bar, he defended the lighter, but superior beer.

When he returned, I continued, "Yeah man, we were on a walk a few months ago when the weather was still warm...first date, girl I met singing karaoke...she was dressed like a damn pirate."

"On your date?"

"No, no, when I met her at karaoke. She was at like a nautical-themed party earlier. When we were walking she told me she worked at a bicycle co-op and I blurted out, 'What are you, some kind of half-assed engineer?' I don't know what I was thinking, for Chrissake."

"Vibe killer?" he asked, and I confirmed. "Damn, I'm surprised...sounds like a good line to me. Reminds me of my great-aunt, she always used to say, 'Shooters shoot.'"

"Smart lady—hey, to your great-aunt." We raised our glasses, then enjoyed big sips of our beers.

* * *

"By the way, you were really ripping today, man," with an empty glass, I complimented.

"Doesn't matter how fast I sail, the horizon's always out of reach," he read the message on his phone. "Alright, you ready to make some moves?"

"Yes, where to?" with uncrossed arms, now sitting up with hands on my thighs.

"Cheese Pocket is at a bar down the road, super close..." as he typed.

"So, you've been there?" I followed.

He looked up, "I may be a creature of habit, but I'll tell you what: I got a lot of habits. This place has the best burgers, they're all about the local meat—should be music there tonight, too."

"Nice—well, I'm finally meeting the Cheese Pocket." I wondered if the cheese wheel was slowing down for Cheese Pocket. Like a game of roulette at the casino, there was a time when Hank's dating was the ball spinning in the opposite direction as the rotating wheel. First, whizzing around the outer edge, passing by all the lucky and not-so-fortuitous numbers, banging his shin on something and then bouncing around like mad. Every time the wheel started to lose momentum, the ball would briefly settle; and like a croupier, he would grab hold and give the wheel a great thrust. A mentally drained gambler at a table for hours, I could not keep all his casual relationships straight.

Though based on our discussion that started at the brewery and continued on the short drive to the bar down the road, I got the sense that his dating had become more subdued, more controlled. With a consolidated approach, the Cheese Pocket had become his main interest in the casino of romance. He kept in touch with a girl that lived near a harbor to which he was often summoned for fishing expeditions. She was the last person he would see before he stepped off of land, and the first person he would see when he stepped back onto land—that is, if he played his cards right. He still had his mobile dating application alias to maintain—though if it were a garden, the vegetables would quickly wither, weeds quickly thrive. When I visited a year before, he had a fully operational farm—woah, where is that chicken from.

In a bright barroom, we sat at a long wooden table. The company included Cheese Pocket and her younger sister. A platonic female friend of Hank's named Eileen was there, too, with a few of her friends. The Cheese Pocket stood up and greeted me with a hug. She was tall, almost my height...surely a bit taller than Hank. Her voluminous breasts made me feel like a frisky teenager. This was not any old hug—this was a hug I thoroughly enjoyed. The Cheese Pocket had a rack!

"Mm, that *is* a tasty burger!" I stated as we began to eat. I could not help myself. When I was younger, half the words I spoke were quotes from *Pulp Fiction*. I liked this quote because there was a chance that someone would recognize the derivation—and if no one did, well, an enthusiastic show of appreciation for a cheeseburger felt like fitting dining etiquette—a mid-meal salute to a common culinary item.

From across the table, I locked eyes with Cheese Pocket's sister—Little Pocket, if you will—who smiled at the remark with her untouched burger held in both hands. With my mouth politely closed, I chewed as we shared this curious moment—though there might have been a bit of one of the condiments stuck in my mustache. The meal continued. After we ate, her boyfriend arrived. Just like that, she was no longer blinking on the sonar device of the ship I was steering. At the helm, no sign of life on the surface.

With elbows on the table, Cheese Pocket began rolling a cigarette with tobacco by American Spirit. Her process looked meticulous. Like decorating a tree with ornaments, sometimes the slow way is the right way. I asked, "Hey, can you roll me one of those, cowboy?" I heard the sonar device beep, another smile from Little Pocket.

She possessed a metallic holder and a stash of rolled cigarettes—she gave me one of those. Into the cold, a few of us went for a quick smoke. "Goddamn, Cheese-y—this is some serious gourmet shit!" praised Hank after his first puff.[34] He called her by name, but I don't recall this title. We talked about her home state, Connecticut, for a while.

Before I moved to New Haven, I went to graduate school in the center of Pennsylvania. As a relatively older student, I studied energy and environmental economics.[35] While writing my thesis, I started rolling my own cigarettes with a spicy flavor called Amsterdam Shag by Peter Stokkebye.

So sophisticated, leaning against the brick wall behind my apartment, I nodded at each passerby as I mulled over the contents of my thesis. Blew a ring of smoke, then breathed deeply through my nose with my eyes closed to honor the thoughts I just completed—then kicked off the wall, and slowly walked to the dumpster, where I put out my cigarette. Up a flight of stairs and through the doorway, now seated at my desk, where a mug of tea was still hot. To a snowy mountain ridge south of State College, I looked out my window. Heading west, a train rode on the near side of the mountain.

When I was a child, my father walked me, my sister, and

a few of our friends along the train tracks by our home—trespassing, really. Their parents were angry with him when they learned of the excursion. Writing a memoir is like walking on train tracks and imagining your younger self coming around the bend, too. Seated at my desk in the center of Pennsylvania, "Alright, back to work, you scabrous dog, and don't wax poetic—this is a graduate thesis and it's serious," as a rule, I thought.

* * *

Cheese Pocket was, of course, an imposed nickname and regretfully the only name by which she'll be remembered here—her real name eludes me now. Before I met the Wet Nurse, another short-lived romance of Hank's—a woman whose name I also don't recall—she would appear as the featured actress in videos he would send on the cellphone application where images and videos vanish upon your watching. Within this social media platform, a group called Shred '19 was formed, composed of the guys we visited in Colorado. One video was particularly memorable.

> *Standing with her back turned to the viewer, the camera began moving downward to her holding up her shirt, to below her waist where she clenched a shoestring French fry with her exposed butt cheeks...then Hank entered the screen from the right, stage left: "Mm, yummy!" he exclaimed with a grin. Then, like a bird at a feeder, he pecked the fry out of her ass.*

He met the Wet Nurse on a work assignment in North

Carolina; together, they cared for sea turtles. Loggerhead turtles were the popular variety in this vicinity, the coasts along the Western Atlantic Ocean—their nests ranged as far north as North Carolina. With changing climates and warming oceans, maybe sea turtles will be nesting in New Jersey while we are still alive. They broke up when she informed him that she was considering the pursuit of a career in prostitution. "Prostitution, how about that?" I responded.

"Yeah man, not too chill," he agreed. I had one environmental occupation—this job was my favorite. I was excited every time I saw a message come through requesting my services, so to speak. Summer down the shore, I was between the years of graduate school. I worked collecting data for my thesis and had plenty of free time for a side gig. Nine and twenty years was my age. I walked into a local kayak shop in sweatpants and sandals, unprepared for an impromptu interview—an open position as a kayak-riding eco–tour guide could fill my free time.

> Lonesome call of the train,
> Cutting through a dark night—
> Shining that lonesome light.
> Lonesome whistle of the bird on the bay,
> Looking for its prey,
> Low is the tide, low is the tide.
> This is where the train rolled.
> We carved a ripple as we carved at the marsh,
> With discretion used in years of war—
> A long time before,
> They ran rum through the river, many years before—

Lonesome call of the train,
On dismantled tracks, vanishing to the stars.
This is where the train rolled—
Vanishing to the stars,
Hear that train's final call from afar.

I wrote these song lyrics about a site we would pass on our kayak tours. As the song implied, a train would carry people from Philadelphia to Atlantic City, then from Atlantic City down the shoreline—these train tracks were dismantled at the water's edge. Through an overgrowth of bayberry and other marshy flora, the train tracks were visible; and metaphoric of an abrupt ceasing of human evolution with Mother Earth idly waiting.

"Come on, let's go, bub," I would say to the squeamish children, afraid to mount the kayak from the dock. I was reading *Sometimes a Great Notion* by Ken Kesey that summer —beast of a novel, 160,000 words. The older brother in the story's gyppo logger group called his younger brother "Bub." *Never give an inch* was the stubborn, masculine motto of the family. To arouse courage within the youngsters, I deployed tough love.

A literary critic compared the prose of a writer to the exhalation that comes after a sip of whiskey—the review was either referring to Kesey or Hemmingway. Perhaps my prose is like the breath that follows a gulp of a frozen Piña Colada. *Ran rum through the river, many years before*—in this lyric, I recalled the bootlegging trade maintained by gangsters dealing with liquor for consumption ten miles north, in Atlantic City. The HBO show *Boardwalk Empire* dramatized this time period; the character Jimmy Darmody would continually toast "to the lost"—took me a while to realize he was paying tribute to the Lost Generation, of which he was a fellow. From time spent in the traumatizing trenches opposing Paul Bäumer and the Axis Powers, Jimmy Darmody was a lost soul, an apathetic shell of himself throughout the show. "To the lost."

"To smoking out the bees, to get the honey from the trees," Hank raised his glass of beer and we all followed. He turned to Cheese Pocket and clanked her glass. Using the same cellphone application that documented the edible experiment featuring the Wet Nurse, Hank snapped a photograph of the Cheese Pocket which earned her name. To Shred '19 he sent a picture of her in jean overalls pinching a piece of sliced cheese—with her fingers. I was not sure if the slice was going into her pocket or coming out of her cheese pocket.

* * *

In the often-overlooked state of Connecticut, I resided. Toad's Place—a night club "where the legends play"—located in New Haven, set between Boston and New York City, offered an opportune pitstop for a band to briefly slow down their tour. Like Argentina and Brazil, the continental giants of South America—what about Chile? Peru? Colombia? While at Lawson's, before we went to the bar down the road, Hank filled me in on a trip from which he had just returned. "So, how was Ecuador?" I asked and he excitedly began.

"I flew into the capital city, Quinto, with a boating buddy named Chris. We took buses and taxis down to Baeza, then Tena and Banos...was like a semi-circle around the westernmost part of the Amazon Rainforest. Each drive took a few hours, and the trip was probably about four hundred miles altogether—and the public transportation is fucking excellent down there. The taxis were pickup trucks, so we could throw our kayaks in the back...and they were affordable taxis.

"Rio Pastaza and Rio Napo, those were the rivers we hit...mammoth tributaries of the Amazon River. Before we left Quinto, we bought boats...we later sold them in Manta, where we flew back from...I actually profited a few shekels." He rubbed his thumb on his pointer and middle fingers and took a sip.

"But we lived in the jungle, dude...we spent our days on the river and set up camp on the riverbanks...fished our meals a few nights and had dried meat and fruit and canned goods during the day. We only paid for shelter the first night in Quinto...needed to orient ourselves and gameplan.

"Wild stuff, man...beautiful, gorgeous, terrifying...I don't know what else to say, you're the words guy." He smacked his hand on the book atop the table, took another swig of beer, then used the back of his hand to remove foam from his beard.

"Kings, man, that's how we felt when we finally arrived at the beach...South Pacific Ocean, six hundred miles away from the Galapagos Islands. They use our dollar down there, but a dollar goes six hundred miles too...we felt like gods, and we ate and drank like kings.

"We were in Manta for two nights...we chilled on the beach during the day, just bronzin'...and that's where I slept too. I may be ragged, but I'm right...things have been going pretty well with the Cheese Pocket, so no ladies for me on this trip...but my friend Chris slept with a girl he met down there in Manta...he almost refused to get on the damn plane to go home."

As he told me about his trip, I was filled with wonder. Victor Frankenstein travels on horseback for a while, then walks beside a mule through the valley of Chamonix. With fervor, Hank told his tale. Mary Shelley was a brilliant writer who imaginatively penned the journey of Frankenstein. A green novelist writing with a questionable and inconsistent punctuative styling—that is what I am—doing my best to recount his journey.

I am enjoying this enterprise—writing is fulfilling and a complement to my primary labor. If I did not have this endeavor, I might be frustrated by unutilized creative capacity. I would likely blame my employer for inadequately occupying my productive time—as though that would be fair. As a guitarist, when you visit a music shop, and pick up and play a beautiful guitar, a whole life of new stories to tell appears in a blaze of energy. I have enjoyed pouring out creative energy though writing, this unfamiliar enterprise.

When four years of work had passed in the earliest stage of my career, my interest in the corporate life began to wither—and like DiCaprio, I scoured the internet in a fit of wanderlust—discovered a portal to an international organization of organic farms that would compensate their migrant workers with the rewarding opportunity of living a sustainable, agrarian life. At lunch with coworkers, I told them about the organization—how I was thinking of booking a one-way plane ticket to Italy. I could pick olives or grapes. "You want me to shovel cow shit?" Fuck it—later, I'll submerge myself in the Mediterranean Sea—will pour a glass of red wine with a heavier hand than usual.

But a miniature sabbatical was all I could devise and execute—a few weeks in Italy, Paris, and Barcelona. Searching for his figurative sword, a wayfaring Paulo Coelho walked the Road to Santiago.[36] In this pivotal moment, with a tantalizing spasm of wanderlust, I took the easy road. How do you keep your spasms of wanderlust at bay?

* * *

We purchased a four-pack of beer at Lawson's and met the Pocket. The air was freezing outside, so, in his trunk, we stowed the beer for later. We were at the bar down the road; and damn, I was starting to get tired. Pitch black when I woke up that morning, crossed the border into Massachusetts at around six of the clock—crossed the state line into Vermont at around seven. Hours after that, I pulled into the resort. I closed my eyes earlier, rested on a bench for a while.

At the bar, he stood. I walked up to my sincere friend. With my right hand, I grabbed ahold of his left shoulder and recited, "Hanky boy, show me the way to go home, I'm tired and I want to go to bed."[37]

He turned to me and revealed a grin, "Ya had a little drink about an hour ago, and it went straight to your head? Hey Cheese Pocket, roll me and Zeno up a few Cheese Pocket Specials—we're blowing this goddamn popsicle stand."

* * *

With my father, I vacationed for a week in Italy. After

he departed from Florence, I was by myself for a few days in Cinque Terre. Temporarily, I sojourned in a hostel, slept in the lower bunk below a stranger. Each morning, the stranger left before I awoke. Every evening, I arrived after the stranger had fallen asleep. After I hiked every inch of trail there was in the park at Cinque Terre, I was satisfied, eager to meet my sister and cousin up in Paris. In Ecuador, Hank ate royally; and in Paris, we did about the same. Via train to Barcelona, we then journeyed. For almost a month, I lived in Europe...a short sabbatical. An ephemeral set-up at a commune in Vermont, that was where peripatetic folks like my friend lived for a while, but when?

Deep in the forest, he lived in a multi-unit home, akin to a commune...way off the beaten track. It was off the track that was off the beaten track. At this time—call it three years ago—where were you? Over and over again, did you gladly rediscover places you've been to before? How did you suppress spasms of wanderlust? Contentedly, somehow.

7

Make My Funk the P-Funk

In New Haven, Connecticut, I fittingly put my master's degree to use as an economist for the parent company of the local electric utility. Sounds like fun, right? The job required charismatic public speaking skills and a diplomatic mindset I did not possess. Like Demosthenes who ridiculed Alexander the Great from Athens, or Cicero who derided Julius Caesar in the same manner, I represented the utility in an ambassadorial forum focused on regional electricity market rule changes in New England. In a quasi-political setting, I would have to speak up in agreement or disagreement regarding market changes that impacted how much people paid for electricity. The work was at odds with my skills, my general nature. You see, I am reticent, or quietly analytical about certain matters, such as the goals contained within this book—easier said than done, and easier written than said. Yes, sometimes I would rather write than speak—and in professional settings, I would rather allow data do the persuasive talking.

But before I moved to New Haven for work—around the time when I went off to graduate school—that was when Hank relocated to Vermont. He once lived in a commune, and sometime after that he bought land south of the city of Burlington—a handful of acres not yet interconnected to the electricity grid of New England. He had plans to inhabit the plot…ah yes, plans to inhabit the plot.

> **Master Sun:** *He changes his actions and revises his plans so that people will not recognize them. He changes his abode and goes by a circuitous route, so that people cannot anticipate him.*
>
> **Zhang Yu:** *When people never understand what your intention is, then you win. The Great White Mountain Man said, "The reason deception is valued in military operations is not just for deceiving enemies, but to begin with for deceiving one's own troops, to get them to follow accordingly.*[38]

* * *

Over the years, I kept in touch quite well with this legend of a man. If there was an event in which the other would be interested, the prospect of our mutual attendance would prompt communication. Yes, we upheld a fairly continuous flow of communication while other friends were more rooted, settling down. And even though we were a couple of rolling stones, we always had a rough idea of the other's whereabouts. So my phone was like a talisman, a totem in my pocket symbolizing the possibility of adventure.

Along the lake waterfront that outlines Burlington, an annual jazz festival takes place...and once upon a goddamn time, he informed me that the festival was *this upcoming weekend, you funky motha trucka!* George Clinton—a member of Parliament Funkadelic—and his band were the main act of the opening evening. During our college years, Parliament Funkadelic was a band that we both appreciated. *"Make my funk the P-Funk, I want to get funked up!"* Make my jazz the— no, that doesn't work. On a weekday in June, Hank told me about this approaching event.

During my senior year at university, we cobbled together a daytime shindig that we called Springfest, which was a tradition that had ceased a few years prior to our attending the school. So this was the reincarnation of the event. From our dark, cavernous basement, rock bands emerged to perform in Hank's backyard, on a sunny afternoon. Bernie Worrell—of Parliament Funkadelic and the Talking Heads—had a show that evening at the Chameleon Club in Lancaster City. Otto reached out to Bernie's manager to request his attendance at the Spring Festival Reincarnation—ten miles away, in the glorified hamlet of Millersville. Amazingly, Bernie showed up— in our eyes, he was a real celebrity, a living legend. Bernie was hard of hearing—and my band did not play softly, nor did the talented group that performed after us, Chaos Thompson. I shook Bernie's hand, hesitantly—did not want to cause any harm to something so sacred. The laudatory remarks that accompanied my handshake were surely unheard. George

Clinton—Bernie's bandmate—was the final act up in Burlington on Friday. On Wednesday, Hank reached out, "Dude, you *gotta* come!" So the plan was decided. Hank was a convincing person—anyone would consider buying his snake oil.

With over two hundred miles of distance between Burlington—a beautiful town, pristinely situated up in a green and mountainous part of the country—and New Haven—which is situated down in the more heavily inhabited delta of New England—well, the trek was not short. But the logistical plan was brought into form. A train runs up there, directly north —to Essex Junction, just east of Burlington—and leaves at one o'clock in the afternoon. This was the mode of transportation I chose to employ to get my ass up to Burlington. I booked a one-way ticket because Hank would be heading south on Sunday. He had a commercial fishing assignment that would launch from Cape May, in the great state of Southern New Jersey. With Connecticut en route, he could cart my ass right back down to New Haven after we made our weekend a funking good, P-Funk time.

From my apartment in New Haven, I frequently heard a steam whistle call of a train. Bathing in the shower, with water vapor escaping from the window, a sonic ripple—a summoning echo through the neighborhood—would penetrate that same open window and combine with the steam in the bathroom air. Quarter to five in the afternoon, church bells rang in the key of C from a block north, summoning nearby Catholics. If my guitar was close, I would pick her up, and along with the bells, I would play—the key of C.

Upon finishing work and with a filled pack on my back, I walked a mile south to the Union Station, in downtown

New Haven. The train was called the Vermonter, and rather than four hours via automobile, the locomotive trek took seven. My spatial and temporal intuitions were pretty strong, though I couldn't explain to you why the damn train dropped me off at Essex Junction at 8:30 p.m.—late considering the departure at one of the clock. But because I enjoyed reading while seated in public transit, taking comfort in being on a predetermined route, I guess I didn't care too much. On the train, I decidedly lost track of time as well. I was reading a novel called *Less Than Zero* by Brett Elliot Easton, a tale of sex and drugs in Los Angeles. Still, performing this first part of the journey in less than seven hours would have been preferred; but again, I was not too bothered. After all, this was a vacation of sorts. In the café car, I sat, drank one overpriced beer, and recalled the train-riding enthusiast my father and I encountered on the Southwest Chief.

From the train, I dismounted and lit up a cigarette. That's right, as I waited for a bus to take me to downtown Burlington, I smoked that cigarette right down to the goddamn filter. I rolled cigarettes at the time, but that cigarette was factory produced. A stale pack of Camel Blues—a favorite of Wayne's, wild son-of-a-gun—was left in the brain pocket of my backpack. The bus picked me up, and a few other travelers, including a middle-aged lady who was going to a story-writing retreat. Does her story tell of the young man who joined her then? As a green novelist himself, he inquired with interest about her upcoming experience. Across the aisle of the bus, an older woman sat and really enjoyed the ride. She waited for the writers' discussion to fade. Then, as a local sage, she explained sites as we passed them. The little town of Winooski really appeared pleasant.

The old sage directed me with pedestrian lefts and rights which would take me to the waterfront concert. When I exited the bus, I could hear the music playing in the distance. So, immediately, I erased her directions from my mind—every infinitesimal square root of a fraction of a millimeter of mental capacity is needed. When the figurative locomotive jostles the figurative luggage stored above, one just hopes every important thing stays put—memories, logical arguments, how to conjugate verbs in Spanish.

Like the child inching her way through the wardrobe to Narnia, I followed the ambient music to the waterfront. In the meantime, Hank sent me a text message—he scouted a breach in the festival security, ajar like a casement window in a bathroom.

Many years ago, we rolled out orange fencing for Springfest, the quite penetrable party. For entrance, we required a ten-dollar cover charge, a much greater deterrent than our flimsy fence. The money we raised would go to a cause chosen by Carl Magoin, Esquire, later known as Ricky Booty Sweat. "Ricky Booty Sweat oh shit!" he exclaimed a few months after the spring festival when we celebrated our graduation in Atlantic City, New Jersey.

After a victorious trip to the casino that weekend, Carl, flush with cash—perhaps 120 dollars or so—indulged himself with a professional massage the following morning. A few years before, Carl's father passed away. We collected money for the purpose of researching his late father's illness. We raised over a thousand dollars, a noble sum for a bunch of selfish college kids. Though more importantly—in my opinion—on that day, fun was had by all.

At that time, I was romantically involved with a girl named Cassidy who was studying at Pittsburgh. We met when she was visiting her hometown friend in Millersville. Her friend was Hank's girlfriend, the Tarantula. What an unflattering nickname, eh? At Springfest, we were blessed with a blue-sky, sun-shining kind of day. I recall Cassidy lying on her back on a terribly constructed, drink-serving bar table that was brought up the stairs from Hank's basement to the backyard...and a friend pouring liquor shots in her mouth—Peach Schnapps—a frequent purchase by Hank Bellefonte.

Cassidy was attractive—Pennsylvanian, but with an exotic, worldly aura. At Duquesne University, she studied economics. For a dork like me, that was an appealing characteristic. Cassidy drove an old, box-like BMW sedan, surely from the eighties. She had short blonde hair and was the only girl with whom I smoked a cigarette in bed after the intercourse of sex.

Months later, Cassidy visited me at my parents' home, when I had the house to myself. We ate burritos for dinner. On her kissable upper lip, a piece of rice was stuck, which I pointed out. Without a remark and with one swipe of her finger, she found the grain, then adhered it to the wall. She was cute, and she was a quirky one; and evidently, she had a nonchalant, artistic way. So memorable was that grain of rice, it still decorates a wall at a restaurant in my mind. With Cassidy, I could dine there today if I would like—cargo unjostled, for now.[39] We raised over a thousand dollars, a noble sum; but more importantly, on that day, fun was had by all. Apologies for the repetition—maybe I hit a bump in the train tracks! *¡hablo español pero no hablo bien!*

At most parties, Hank contributed a bottle of Peach Schnapps. The beer we drank was never of a high standard. Keystone—Genesee Cream Ale—Natural *Natty* Light, or Ice. About Disaronno, Hank told me an utterly absurd story—so brace yourself. An endorsement was offered in his introduction, "Dude, you should *definitely* try Disaronno." This was a heartfelt recommendation, spoken with gravitas. The story involved childhood friends of his—twin brothers and a few girls...and was set during a winter break between semesters in our third year at university.

From a bottle of Disaronno, they drank. On that evening, the small party collectively realized the extent to which Disaronno was delicious. This was one of those sophisticated times when adulthood flashes right before you—like the moment when one looked upon themself in the bathroom mirror at the bar after a few of their first legal alcoholic beverages—smiling, even just for a fleeting moment, they do not feel so goddamn juvenile.

So they started discussing pornography. "What a *great* way to make money, ehh?" a twin suggested, and the girls agreed. In a sexual medley, they all proceeded. With the girls going at it in the open, Hank filmed the event. He received his own private experience in another room—and ever since then, Hank highly recommended and probably still recommends to this day, "Wait, *definitely* try Disaronno."

* * *

Time elapsed between his reconnoitering and my late

arrival, and the breach in the jazz festival security sealed up; but I found an alternative entrance. With the exchange being a relinquishing of the right to purchase and drink alcohol, a man was letting a mass of people bypass the hour-long line. He indicated this deal with an X marked on the back of one's hand; but I was in, and Hank joyously welcomed me. To his friends I was immediately introduced. Giving me more credit than I deserved, he cheered, "This is my friend Zeno, he *snuck* in! This sneaky son of a bitch snuck in!"

His buddies were fellow lift operators employed by the Arbol de Azucar Mountain Resort, located about an hour south of Burlington. Oliver was either British, American with a speech impediment, or on psychedelic drugs—maybe two or three of those possibilities. He was young and studying at the university in Burlington. I also met a couple that lived at the Mad River Junction, well outside of town in the Green Mountain country. The girl was attractive, and the guy was cool—and we all stayed at a campground that evening along the waterfront. To chop wood for the fire, he used a hatchet.

Hank's new love interest was an old acquaintance, Suzie Le'Song—please pay attention as I proceed. She was a Millersville Marauder that had just moved to Vermont after a stint in Las Vegas; and before that, she lived somewhere in South Carolina...before that, Arizona. A lot of distance between those three homes. To Suzie, leaving came naturally. Suzie was the mother, owner of a cat—and as a hobby, like a cat, or some other animal adept at traversing difficult terrain, she climbed up natural walls of rock. She also skied, and once let me borrow her pass card for a few runs on a lazy day at the slopes. So Suzie was hospitable, and also agreeable—to matters in which she concurred, her instinctive reaction was the expression, "*Fuck* yee*eaah*!"[40]

At the festival, I drank one beer and had about two thirds of a second beer—ignorantly, I did not catch this *X*-mark stipulation. It was a mad *river* rush in through the gate, and the security guard marked the *X* on my hand quickly. To about thirty minutes of funk music I listened, and then the same guy that *mad river* ushered me in found me enjoying a beer. He grabbed the cup out of my hand and on the ground, he tossed the remainder of the drink. "Ah, what a waste," I thought while looking him in the eye. The show was finishing up soon anyway, so this wastefulness and early exit were not too big of a big deal. Outside the perimeter of the music area, I set my backpack down in the grass and waited. Not too much time passed before Hank and the merry lift operators met up with me.

We walked up the cliffside back toward the center of town where the bus had dropped me off a short while ago. I carried my backpack. Hank pushed along his mountain bike.

"So, where are we going?" asked I.

"We are on our way to Nectar's," replied Hank.

"Ah, you know about Nectar's, right? That's the bar that hosted Phish in their formative years...when they studied at the University of Vermont." I liked the band, was obsessed for a while. A miracle I have not brought this up yet...and Hank was not a fan—and in this matter, and perhaps this matter only—he was quite full of shit.

"I fuckin' hate Phish," he repeated.

"Dude, you're full of shit!" Yes, we had this conversation before...

"They suck, man—*give the director a picture of nectar*, I get it."[41]

"You don't know what you're talking about! I agree with you on a lot of things, man—damn near everything—but on this matter, you are full of shit!" I said.

Suzie—again, an agreeable person overall—disagreed in the matter of Hank's harsh judgement of the band Phish. "I'm of the opinion that *Phish* is not the *only* topic about which Hank is full of shit," she joked. When Hank moved in with Suzie and witnessed firsthand the feline-litter-box-shitting approach, I am sure that—for mirth—he drove a debate for the right to adopt the same maneuver. On the porcelain, he would settle...but decided that—to make visitors feel at home —he would offer the litter box as an option for defecation. "Yes, make yourself at home...the litter box is right here, next to the couch."

On a couch, surrounded by friends, with my acoustic guitar on my lap, this was the setting of some of my favorite musical moments. Premeditating an arrangement consists of a quick confirmation of a chord progression and assigning vocal responsibilities—we would embark in song and look forward to the part where we jammed. In my righteous opinion, the members of Phish were as adventurous as musicians could be—they wielded their instruments like Hank careening down rapids on his kayak...then taking a break to float along a pristine stream slowly, blissfully. They are past their prime, they are getting older—but like crossing a group of old guys hiking up a mountain, the joy is so apparent as they ascend.

* * *

Once we summitted the cliff that rose above the waterfront concert area, we walked toward Church Street—a busy pedestrian pathway with restaurants, bars, stores, movie theaters with marquees. There is no Ferris wheel on Church Street…he ran toward me years ago, holding something mysteriously—but during the holiday season, there is a decorated tree that stands magnificently at the top of the avenue. With night owls, the street was buzzing.

An hour before midnight was the time, and some of Hank's other pals were already at the bar. We wanted to get there more rapidly than could be achieved on foot. So I hopped on the seat of his bike with my backpack, which held my belongings for the weekend—a tent, sleeping bag, clothing, headlamp, a medicine bag, and some food. While I held onto two fistfuls of his shirt to balance, he rode his bike standing. We carved in and out of people on this crowded street, going slightly downhill. "Look out!" "Get the fuck out of the way!" and maybe even a "Move it or lose it!" were all exclaimed as we journeyed toward Nectar's…the home of a chandelier that coincidentally resembles the stamen of a flower, and the home of—well, you know—the *legendary* musical group, Phish.

The pedestrian pathway was crowded, and we were surely disobeying a minor law that prohibited our mode of travel. Hank realized we were approaching a cop, stood off to the right. He muttered, "Oh shit!" Then, as if in a video game with a controller and joystick, the bike quickly jolted left. He steadied the vehicle, now on the other side of the street, then pressed the goddamn acceleration button.

Skidding to a stop, with the back wheel dragging and whipping out to the side for effect, we reached our destination. We entered, turned the corner to the barroom to find a rock band playing. Immediately, a gay guy started hitting on Hank; eventually, Hank had to break the news of his heterosexuality to him. From afar, I observed this suitor come on strong, and then he pivoted his fixation to me. Now I was the central target of his powerful advance. At first, his forward and overt nature was astounding. I was less welcoming of this flirtation, "I don't want to waste your time or my time—I'm not gay." Thankful and unfazed, a man on pursuit, he then dawdled off for a new target.

"Phew, that was wild," blurted out Hank. Suzie compared our experience to the common romantic overtures of aggressive men which she had, of course, experienced. She gave off a scintillating aura, she was pretty—dark hair and green eyes. Her comparison opened our eyes, so to speak.

After a chunk of time equivalent to two or three Fiddlehead IPAs, Suzie arranged a ride to the North Street Beach campground along Lake Champlain. Hank rode his bike to meet us there—earlier, prior to my arrival, Hank and his friends set up camp. In the dark and in the small hours of night, we arrived. In a small field surrounded by woods, by a carved-out path leading to the lake, the campsite was...above the encircling tree line, a clear night sky. I picked a star and set up my tent.

* * *

She was the craziest character of them all and she accompanied us that weekend, too. At our university, she was a younger pupil, and her name was Amelia. One day I will put down the proverbial pen that writes all of this; and in the meantime, I am trying to be as respectful as possible—who knows which hands this book will encounter. In these sensitive times, any criticism must be prefaced with some kudos. Amelia was *so* wacky that I was thankful to see her about once every two years, just to remind myself *how* goddamn wacky she was...that's not necessarily a denigrating remark, right?

At university—when we were collocated Marauders and ran into each other more frequently—her eyes would first bulge, then she would balance herself like a seasick pirate, reciting a long story about what just happened to her. I thought her head was going to pop when I asked her, "If you're always telling stories, when do you find time to make new ones?"

To New Hampshire, she relocated. She possessed a dog that behaved as poorly as she could. Putting this puppy aside—and despite her being a damn lunatic worth observing biannually —she was fun, energetic, and not too absorbed in her image to play, so to speak. With her, she brought rollerblades which were *rad*, as she proclaimed. If you asked her if she was any good at skiing, she would say she was excellent and use profanity for emphasis; but Hank disagreed and opined, "Dude, she sucks, she thinks she's the 'Ski Queen of the East.'"

"Dude, she can really move!" I never skied with her.

"Move? She takes the rock out of a rocking chair."

Hank lent me his rollerblades the following day and the three of us rolled along the waterfront pathway. Amelia had an incredible wipe-out; she performed the classic fall. She rode a declining curve too widely, and rolled onto the bumpy macadam where she lost her center of gravity. Leaning back, her roller blades flew forward, her legs swung upward, and her body completely left the ground. Her arms waved back behind her head, and she fell directly on her ass. I thought that type of shit only happened in cartoons.

In the moonlight of the prior evening, we arrived at the campground. I was ready to tucker out promptly after my tent was prepared. Hank irritated his girlfriend throughout the evening—bicycling in a roundabout way, he returned to the campground after much time ticked, the final straw. The issue I recall was that he was not very communicative throughout the evening, and he left her hanging with the "where's" and "when's." But with intimate relationships, I've read that conflict stimulates growth.

Anyway, blocs formed...well, Amelia allied with Suzie, and Hank was on his own. Amelia likely decided her position in order to directly participate in any ensuing drama—she and Suzie were friendly, but not close friends.

When I was a senior at university, a truly close friend of Suzie's had a crush on me. I lived in the big room of a party house which had an appealing effect on my female classmates, like Otter's suite in *Animal House*. My large bedroom was furnished poorly. In the corner of the room, I rested on a dinky twin bed that awkwardly left plenty of openness in the rest of the space. My guitar amplifier was placed in another corner to the right upon entry and stood about eight feet past the room's threshold. One evening during a party, I was lying in bed and just about to fall asleep in my tiny bed—too drunk to continue socializing, too absent to appreciate and thank the giver of oblivion; and oblivion was where I was heading. With a thunderous boom, the door flew open and Otto fell forward. He launched himself into my tall amp. A neon light shaped as a guitar placed on top came crashing down on him as he yelled, "Gah!" He lifted himself up from the wreckage and forced me to create a spot for him in the little bed, all unbeknownst to the party-goers downstairs who likely did not flinch. Suzie's friend wondered, "Have you seen Zeno?"

Lying in my tent, not asleep just yet, I listened to the commotion of Suzie and Amelia seizing Hank's truck. If the squabble was not due to an earlier feud regarding poor communication, perhaps there were simply not enough sleeping provisions for all. Hank conceded his vehicle for their return home, which would be perhaps the quarter millionth mile recorded on his old truck.

To observe the departure, I unzipped the door to my tent. Suzie attempted to drive the truck up a steep grade, but she lacked momentum and could not surmount the hill—the wheels began to spin like Amelia with her goddamn roller blades. Again, she went for the climb like a second pinball in the machine, and conquered the hillock, bounced off a star, then drove off and away from the campsite. I zipped up my tent, marked the page in this story of life I've lived, and then went to sleep.

* * *

I woke up early in a hot tent—you know that feeling—to a beautiful morning, but to an upset stomach. During this stage in life, I cut back on drinking liquor to nearly never; and every other day, I drank mushroom tea instead of a daily pot of coffee. I swear to God that that improved my digestive system—go figure.

While I slept, Hank rode his bike to Suzie's apartment in the twilight of the night. With thirst and an ailing stomach, I packed up my belongings and schlepped them down through the path to the lake, to the walkway along the waterfront. One step at a time, I trudged along toward downtown Burlington. I appeared more interesting than I was. "Hey, where are you backpacking from!?" strangers inquired. I responded, "Oh no, I rode the train here from Connecticut!" Along this queasy perambulation, I arranged lyrics to a new song.

> Even if the sky flew away, or fell down the ground—
> If the moon and stars slipped out of their spots,
> And started swirling around—
> Blue sky shining like the golden sun,
> Or like clouds floating alone—
> Shooting star, like an outlaw on the run,
> Turn around, go back home.
> Smoke from fire up in the clouds, every time I'm mad—
> Rains from forests ablaze, each time that I'm sad—
> Drought turning life to dusty death,
> They'll never forget that canyon hole—
> Monsoons from afar find the river,
> Flood the city of my soul.
> These words are like seeds in soil,
> One day there will be flowers around my home.

Slowly, I journeyed to the neighborhood known as Old North End, where Suzie stayed in an upstairs portion of a duplex—her place was next to a cemetery. After typing in the security code which she messaged to me, I walked upstairs and took the home off my back. To coffee, I helped myself and waited a short while—there were a few cups leftover in the pot, but I brewed some more—trusting the leftovers were from the day before, I mixed right in the freshly brewed coffee—vagabonds aren't picky about libation matters such as this...

Amelia must have driven to New Hampshire to take care of her dog—there, she was not. When Hank rose from his slumber and joined me, I tested his memory, "Dude, how about the time when we slept in that cemetery after the beer festival?"

"Here Lies Zeno Francis—Dead as a Doornail—Lived Like a Doinker," he rubbed his eyes, replied, and then laughed to himself.

"Hank Bellefonte—Went Fishin'—Ran Out of Bait," the ghost of Zeno responded with a smile, then took a sip of coffee. From the cabinet left of the sink, Hank grabbed a mug and looked out the window above the sink, to the graveyard.

"Where there's fish, there's a way," he uttered seriously.

Shortly after Hank and Suzie awoke, we decided to go back to the North Street Beach. First, we packed up her car with a kayak and a large inflatable raft. Before we left, Suzie informed me that her friend Elaine was coming up from Boston for the day and evening. The exciting sensation of a romantic prospect. Like a drug she injected, "She's hot! She's probably my hottest friend, Zeno!"

At around noon, we were the first beachgoers to arrive—then Hank's friends trickled in—first Oliver, then the cool guy with the hatchet, and his girlfriend. A girl that coincidentally dated Carl Magoin recently moved to Burlington, and she joined us—brought her kayak as well. A tiki bar along the beach—there, we got beers and burgers for lunch. Fed, we went back to our spots on the beach. Inflated, the raft was ready for us to paddle our asses out to the rocky cliff off in the distance. Macho, Hank and I tested out the raft. Arriving after noon, Elaine surely was gorgeous. Then, at last, Amelia arrived with her dog.

Elaine was an artist. She went to Millersville, too; but at Millersville, we never met. We discussed this, and we discussed our respective decisions to relocate to New England. She in Boston, and your once beloved narrator, in New Haven. She had a European look and smiled often. Then the four of us—Hank, Suzie, Elaine, and yours truly—climbed aboard the raft and took off for the cliff. Like a couple of Venetian gondola drivers, Hank and I stood and paddled. I began to sing, "On top of sphagh*eeeeeee*tti, all covered with cheese!" Hank laughed, then harmonized.

The ride was a successful out-and-back, though it was a hard effort that neither Hank nor I were going to admit. For me, this struggle had a clear payoff—a way to illustrate my masculinity to Elaine. Strength would be the linguine. A bit of humor, the parmesan cheese...and having a genuine person like Hank Bellefonte to call a friend, the meatballs. Altogether, a pretty damn debonair combination.

Arriving ashore, we regained our land legs and got one final round of drinks from the tiki bar. After we devised a plan for dinner, Suzie and Elaine left to prepare for the evening. With cleanliness and appearance, Hank and I were less concerned. We had a nice glisten from the activities of the day and we hoped to maintain it. Amelia booked a campsite, though

I'm not sure if anyone stayed there that evening—might have been just her and that rambunctious little puppy dog.

She alleged she had been dating someone for a few months. He was apparently a "real ripper," and he may well have been. For dinner, she joined us at a restaurant called Daily Planet—maybe extra company, but her presence was alright because she was a talker, a real goddamn conversationalist that had no time for awkwardness. From across the table, Elaine and I gazed at each other; this time, her smile was coy. We both drowned out the sound. For a long moment, we stared as deeply as we could into each other's eyes. With her lips and her eyes, her smile grew to be more coquettish.

"I'm getting shots, what do we want?" Amelia offered after dinner.

"Disaronno?" Hank suggested, but whiskey from Ireland was what she ordered. I sipped a small amount of the whiskey and partook in the clanking tradition of cheers. "To swimming with bow-legged women," Hank expressed, as an earnest wish before we all drank. I wondered if he knew the essential translation of that toast, "To having sex." I believe he was aware, that crazy son of a bitch.

At a night club down the street from the Daily Planet, music from younger times was played. So, on this day—if you're keeping track—we did not listen to much jazz music at all. Everyone feeling confident, collectively jovial, company being enjoyed by all, we danced until late that evening. And we were all about thirty years old at this point. Hank and I were thirty-one, and as for Suzie and Elaine, perhaps nine and twenty years of age. I did note that I was a "relatively older" graduate student. Did I indicate our age well? That, for us all, time was moving right along...

* * *

Hank was an expert in maintaining vitality. At some point thus far in life, did you gather that your vitality is maintained, or rather needs to be maintained—as if weakness conquers strength? But if you lose your youthful exuberance, I decree it can be rebuilt to some extent. With dedicated effort, one can regain their vitality. Did you ever have that realization? Otto and I hiked up Mount Monadnock in southern New Hampshire. A seemingly healthy, happy, and very elderly woman—a widow perhaps—was foraging at the base of the mountain. In her voice, there was a fascination that was lovely and inspiring. She loved her husband until death did them part...and then she fell back in love with life. Hank always carried youthfulness with him—never lost his vibrance—impervious to the spell cast by time.

Even when he entrenched himself in an anti-government political leaning that could be pugnaciously outspoken, he was still a thoughtful person; anyway, Vermont may be more right leaning than proven by political outcomes of recent history.[42] He was a stranger in this territory. He moved there like it was his destiny. The strangers were attracted to him due to his affability and his animated style of communication. He was interested in them, too, which requires a bit of genial enthusiasm that is more typical of the young in body and heart.

As a sportsman of strictly *extreme* sports, he fit right in up there. Though later that summer, he half broke his neck mountain biking—had to fit his heavy head into one of those hyperboloid neck braces. "I don't know about mountain biking, man—I always hear about mountain bikers getting in gnarly accidents," stated your wandering memoirist. And don't fret—your lead character is in fine, roughly symmetrical form these days.

"Sometimes ya gotta endure a few stings to get to the honey," he reasoned; bear a few stings to enjoy whatever your honey may be—one hell of a sting for some honey. Duane drew a target on the toe of Gregg's moccasin, and before that they drove through a ghetto in Florida to purchase a gun. With an intensifying Vietnam War, the draft for the young and able pursued people like Gregg Allman; but with a musical career also beginning to intensify, the brothers needed a strategy—so Duane shot Gregg's foot.

When they arrived at the hospital, Gregg realized the bloody moccasin—with a bullet hole through a scribbled bull's eye—was clear evidence of his plot to dodge the draft. To the shoe, Gregg discreetly pointed. The bassist quickly removed the proof from the medical room...and the rest is history. A daring strategy that worked. Bold decisionmakers who emphatically played their instruments. *"You were lost in a silver spoon; thought I pulled you out in time"*...just like that, energized for the rest of the day.

Hank was a brave kayaker who never chased waterfalls—waterfalls chased him—really rambling now.[43] Kayaking was his spring and summer sport. During these seasons, he mountain biked as well. In the winter months—when he would nourish himself with venison from a buck he killed with gratitude—Hank focused on skiing. In one wintry season, he skied at Arbol de Azucar on thirty and one hundred separate days. If he skied one hundred times, he would be awarded a "sick hat." How about that for ambition? How about Hank beating the mark by a long shot?

"Happiness isn't on the road to anything. Happiness is the road."[44] The hat was like Coelho's sword in *The Pilgrimage*. Hold on to that thought—wrap the string of the kite around your finger, leave that sick hat out on the table—I will discuss this more in a chapter or two—non-linearity always worked for Tarantino. Back at university, we turned up "Don't Keep Me Wonderin'" so loud the walls vibrated, stomped around the room, jumped, and landed in unison when Duane launched his glass slide up the fretboard—energized for the unpaved path that was the rest of the goddamn day.

Vitality cannot be accomplished in an arrogant manner. Arrogance manifesting as egotism is a desiccating, contrary path to a vitalizing life. Vitality is an individual's agreement to themselves to develop with vigor, where age and death are honored with humbleness every day—holistic health, a perpetual outcome of this procession. While the maintenance of youthful strength and liveliness is the pursuit of an individual, engaging in the broader sphere of sportsmanship is a way to share the tastier fruit of collective vitality.

Seated on a chairlift—ripping cigarettes in our snow gear, with my snowboard dangling from my right foot, zooming forward in more ways than one—to the top of a mountain for our first run of the day. The way he ripped, it seemed he had no limits. But if you were to ask him, "Dude, how do you do it?" he would attribute his vitality to his willing and ready use of, "Well, have you considered gas station boner pills?"

* * *

Suzie's sofa turned into a bed and that is where Elaine and I slept—alternatively, I suppose I could have stayed at the campsite, I had my camping gear—but Elaine and I were digging each other that night. She, Hank, Suzie, and I tore up the dance floor...tore it to pieces. When really feeling the music, I would break out the ancient Egyptian dancer move —at some point we danced like Egyptians in a circle.

* * *

The evening was nostalgic and that's part of the reason why I had to bring up this event—but why nostalgic? With a decade passed, the evening was reminiscent of times when the four of us would approach an evening that same exact way. We were surrounded by unpretentious Marauders, and we could still do it; wait, what is it? As a writer, I try not to use the word "it"—you know, that is one of my guiding rules of this composition.

I received a valuable education at Millersville, and I have done well with my little bachelor's degree. I was taught to refrain from the use of the ambiguous word "it." Hank studied marine biology and was always applying that degree usefully as well. But, more importantly, the culture at Millersville was modest and friendly. Symbolically, two swans lived at the pond in front of the mathematics building, signifying that friendship was possible here—relationships and partnerships could be built patiently and with grace—Miller and S'Ville, the names of the swans.

If preferred, or if by a drunken, boisterous accident,

romantic relations could be made at Millersville. Fueled by alcohol and lust—maybe this evening in Burlington was of that sort—but if that were the case, for Marauders, that was acceptable. I liked Elaine—if she lived around the corner, who knows what could have happened. If she wrote a book about Suzie, maybe she'd have the same thing to say about yours truly.

* * *

Finished work, stocked pack on my back, and walked to the train station in downtown New Haven. The train fare I purchased a few days before was for the trip north to Burlington—through Hartford, Springfield, Brattleboro, Montpelier, and many more towns in between. In reverse and southward down the same line, the daily train left Essex Junction early in the morning—the lonesome train departed after we all awoke, vanished to the stars before we began our day. With bicycles and rollerblades, we traveled across town to a vegan breakfast place. We probably looked like the happiest goddamn imbeciles.

The grand plan was that Hank would drive us south late in the afternoon; but early in the afternoon, the captain beckoned Hank—the trip was delayed a few days; and simultaneously, a contractor coordinated a land survey with Hank—he was available the next day to look at Hank's property. So—just like that—my ride south disappeared, and the solitary train already left the station.

While a unique, polyrhythmic band played in the street, I anxiously mulled over how the hell I was going to get back home. The lead player wielded a peculiar instrument from West Africa called a *ngoni* and overlaid the music with dreamy wistfulness. Anxiety felt like a ridiculous thing to emote. While dancing, we devised one final plan.

Hank would lend me his truck and I would drive alone, southward to New Haven. Hank owned a motorcycle, which was parked on his property. First, we would pick up his motorcycle, and then we would part ways. For his work trip in a few days, he would ride his motorcycle down to New Haven. After picking up his truck, he'd drive the remainder of the journey to Cape May—fairly heroic.

Hank's land contained a stream running down a steep hill to an opening in a wooded area which had an occupant. Hank's friend parked a school bus on the property and was living in squalor. When we arrived, there the bus was, deserted in the middle of the goddamn woods. "You want to check it out?" he asked.

"Ehh, honestly, dude, I'm alright," I responded. We still peeked our heads in for a look—goodness, gracious...Mary, Mother of God, pray for us sinners...

We walked through the forest to the top of the hill. He proposed that the rock formation on this hilltop would be the foundation for which he would construct a deck. He pointed to the trees that would be cleared to create an overlook of the mountain ridge off in the distance. He pointed to where he thought the sun was going to set that night. At last, he pointed to the ground to conclude the scene, "And we'll have our asses parked here in Adirondack chairs one day, like a couple of Tommy fuckin' Bahamas." Over the mountains, the sun set in this beautiful, imaginary vista. Close your eyes—

above the shadows of the ridge, paint the sky lavender and a brilliant pink.

* * *

He gave me the keys and told me he would be heading back to Burlington in a little while; had a chore of some sort to take care of on his property. Fought off anxiety earlier, and now with a feeling of guilt, I drove down the path, a quarter mile to the paved road—a few turns and I was on the highway heading south—I drove for an hour before I checked my phone. The truck's key chain also contained the key to his damn motorcycle—he was stranded![45]

"Dude, I was running after you and yelling like a mad man!" he told me once I returned the missed call. Can't you picture that? When I do, I imagine him wearing clunky rubber boots he would wear on a goddamn fishing boat...He should have taken off a boot to throw at the truck. About halfway between where I had driven to and Burlington, there was a gas station—I drove there and dropped the motorcycle keys off. "My friend is going to pick these up, he's coming from Burlington."

"OK—what does he look like?" she asked.

"Long-ish, golden-brown hair—my age—pretty stout—he's got a beard...he's a real mountain man!" described yours truly.

"What's his name?" to be sure.

"Hank is his name—or you could call him 'Tweak.' He's been known to respond to that, too. Yes, call him "Tweak"...he'd get a kick out of that," said yours truly. You know, I probably would have heard him shouting if I wasn't busy dreaming of lavender sunsets.

***

On his tiny motorcycle, he arrived the next day successfully. Like young collegians recalling a blurred evening that involved the excessive drinking of alcohol, we had an enjoyable recap; yes, we recapitulated some of the details of what happened on that pull-out couch...the couch really allowed for a night of deep, satisfying sleep.[46] Eventually, "Alright, man, when's the next time I'll see ya?" Toward the door, we started walking.

Him responding, "We land a few days before the Fourth of July—let's see—I could stop by on the way back up to Vermont for some New Haven pizza?"

Prolonging from behind, "That's a long trip at sea...what did ya say you're fishing for?"

Answering as he moved forward, "Scallops—yes it is, man—it's good money though—we're going up to George's Bank and back...you've seen *Perfect Storm*?"

"Phew, be careful, man...Yes, but Clooney's got nothing on you—" then realizing, "Ah wait, damn, I'll be down the shore for the holiday—you know, fireworks and shit."

In song, "Why do you build me up—buttercup—just to let me down?" as he opened the door.

"Nice—I'll see ya soon though, brother, drive like the wind," I laughed.

Exiting the apartment, taking the first step down the stairs, "I'll fly like an eagle on the wind," he corrected, chuckling as the door closed.

8

The Long Trail

"A creation of singular beauty...magnificent in its best moments," was the *Washington Post* review of a certain masterpiece.[47] Welcome back from your ocular journey to and from the back of the book. My proficiency as a writer is awful compared to Tolkien—probably shouldn't even be compared, apples to oranges, as they say.

At the University of Oxford, Tolkien was a philologist. By his participation in the first world war of the modern age, he was molded. But in our anthropologic history, Alexander the Great laid siege on all of known humanity, no? On the Yucatan Peninsula, the Mayan civilization peaked centuries after the death of Alexander the Great; perhaps his impact was like a tidal wave that expedited the eastward migration of civilized people. Then upon Spanish occupation, the Mayan history was largely erased due to their refusal to adopt Christianity—with an obliteration of Mayan texts by the Spanish, in retaliation. But from those that partook in this more recent, momentous scrap of extreme injustice and utilization of arms—such as Tolkien—much literature promulgated and is available today. If Tolkien's like a Macoun apple—the best of the apple varieties—then I am like a dried prune. With all due respect to prunes, and those that enjoy them.

My authoring approach is what I termed the Johnny Appleseed Method. I did not have a tree nursery of work to transplant, to grow a forest. On this writing journey, I one day embarked, laying a seed crudely in the ground—and then another, and another. On my path forward, always on the lookout for inspiration—pluck inspiration from air, place that symbolic nugget in my back pocket, and then return to tend to a sapling, a small tree where this rousing snippet would make sense. I still have to tell you what I was doing in Newport—we'll see if I get to that.

"Pretty good in its best moments," an expected review—but I say that, then I recall the simple but effective prose of Kurt Vonnegut, and I say to myself, "Who knows...keep going, man." Vonnegut was a real jackass—I think he'd be happy to hear that review. On one page he's a jackass, and on the next he was my best friend. The smartest writer there ever was, ever will be. That's his opinion. He also would say he stunk, and his readers were morons—played cards intently with partial decks. Albert Einstein read Vonnegut, too. Einstein was pretty smart. Pretty good in its best moments, with this moment flashing by—what do you think, how is this moment? To the end, we are getting pretty close. How is this book going anyway? Did you like the part about the prunes? How about the part where I likened my book to a goddamn cloud in the sky? "How's his book? Is he any good at writing?" they will ask.

"If Tolkien is a ripe, sweet, watery, *delicious* apple...well, he is an apple core decaying in a damn dumpster." How's that for confidence? I'm reminded of the expression "liquid courage"—why most of my stories might involve alcohol...yeast excrement, what a disgrace.[48] No, I think someone will enjoy this damn thing; and my alcohol drinking isn't to overcome timidity. Inveterately, I enjoy the social merriment that a round of beers brings—like the frothy libation is some sort of reward. "Love yourself"—as I'm going through the manuscript and editing my little memoir, I think I like the timbre of my words overall...my voice, the toot of my goddamn horn.

And so—toot, toot—without further ado, I would now like to transcribe some fairly direct kissing and telling. This will be a quick series of my romantic endeavors in New Haven, a few of which were peculiar enough to recount—the tale of the last partner will serve as a smooth segue to the next, final episode.[49] This upcoming section may be juvenile—and for you, torturous even—but Jack Gilbert wrote poems about lovers his whole life...I think I should be able to get away with using a handful of book pages. Anyway, flip the pages to better understand your position—see how much you have read compared to what remains? You really are getting pretty close to the end!

Ha!

Alright—so, in New Haven, I started to feel like Jerry-feckin'-Seinfeld. With each romantic partner, I would unearth some issue...you know the Seinfeld shtick. I was getting rejected at a swell rate, too.

For six whole weeks, Carolina and I dated. The first date that was her idea was a goddamn walk in the park where I was informed we were not a good fit. Carolina was one of the intellectually pompous students studying at Yale University. With that attitude, I was doomed from the start, right? Living among these elite graduate students, nine out of ten people one talks to is in the middle of the same inhalation—a college semester, breathing in information. Holding her breath for a second to break up with me, she was probably correct. Our dissonance was *that* straightforward...we were not a good fit.

Sky occupied herself as a nurse at Yale Hospital. Tiny in stature, she possessed a bright, disproportionately large smile. She windsurfed—and on the third date, I handed her a picture I drew of a windsurfer. She lit up holding that piece of paper. When she looked up at me there was a damn twinkle in her eyes. Sky went skiing one weekend and slept in her Ford Bronco, which I thought was badass. She showed me a picture of her setup, then broke down and told me she went with a coworker she was also dating—she thought she could date multiple people...but she couldn't do the charade anymore.

I've tried the overlap, too. Playing the field can be hard to gracefully execute, or exit. The "open relationship" concept was intriguing. I read up on the arguments for the benefits of consent in an "open relationship" and I was not compelled. A partner should be given ample space, I understood that but was not convinced that they should fill that space with more romanticism. Simultaneously, I would be filling that space, too. Was I supposed to read a damn magazine? Should I develop other romantic alliances with the time? Seems like a convoluted path to agree to walk on—I would prefer one tortured path of partnership rather than a network of trails in a park of love. The monogamous simplicity just seems more peaceful—otherwise, I would probably get lost in the woods.[50]

* * *

Cyan put my heart in a damn food processor, or that might have been my honor she pureed. At a coffee shop during a meditation event, the two of us met. A graduate student from California spread the love to us cold northeasterners. After the meditation, there was a group discussion about love, "Is it an issue to not love your work?" and "What does love *look* like?" In a sharing mood, I recalled a sensation of sorts from years ago, which was experienced down the shore—the Venice to my being Casanova.[51]

Very late in the afternoon, when the sun tints the world amber, I walked along the water with waves crashing on my ankles, with sandpipers running to and fro. I came across a girl with whom I worked for a few summers...and on whom I had a crush. She was four years my junior—a few too many at the time of our mutual employment. At a party with my previous coworkers, our first and only kiss occurred. I was three and twenty years of age...this was a year or two after my working at the Surf Mall.

In our spare time between shifts, these coworkers and I gallivanted across the island. After I moved on and was more gainfully employed, we still kept in touch and got together on weekends in the summer. Shortly before the kiss, I had smoked a cigar. We walked down to a damp, sandy area by the bay. We sat and our lips finally embraced. Between the taste of tobacco smoke, the unpleasant smell of the salty bay with exposed and decaying marine life in the low tide, our moistening ass cheeks...she was probably disgusted, for Chrissake. Crashing into her on the beach that amber afternoon, an ether changing to satin by the second, where "the sun was glowing, shining off her...and everything behind her became a wondrous haze." At the coffee shop, this was how I responded to the question of love and what love might look like...

> ...following the bird under the shadow of the trees he passed deep into Nan Elmoth and was lost. But he came at last to a glade open to the stars, and there Melian stood; and out of the darkness he looked at her, and the light of Aman was in her face. She spoke no word; but being filled with love Elwë came to her and took her hand, and straightway a spell was laid on him, so that they stood thus while long years were measured by the wheeling stars above them, and the trees of Nan Elmoth grew tall and dark before they spoke any word.[52]

From across the circle, I confidently spoke my inner thoughts. The coffee shop embodied a special atmosphere that made one feel comfortable revealing their true identity. A place where average people transformed to above average. I did not realize my answer intrigued Cyan—but did she want to be my sunflower, or a flower fixed upon another sun? Waiting in an urban forest like Melian, stunning a wandering man in his tracks with the beauty of her appearance. Cyan was sexy with a devious, alluring appearance...like a young Megan Fox.

A group of us had become regular patrons at the coffee shop, and Cyan and I were like Ross and Rachel.[53] To a bar down the street one evening, the gang ventured. Both standing, leaning against the bar, she revealed, "I'm surprised you've never asked me out!?" So now please let me explain my sad hypothesis about how I ultimately misinterpreted this remark.

Some semblance of a summer fling followed her observation. Cyan's friends owned a motorboat, and at the Thimble Islands—a few times during our fling—we dropped anchor. They were fun days during the first summer that I lived in Connecticut, but her friends were moronic boatsmen. A mishap every trip, I wish I could tell you about them all. On one windy day, the captain tossed inflatable tubes into the sound as if the body of water were a contained swimming pool. In the current and wind, the tubes immediately drifted...the captain jumped in and chased after them. Without a first mate, the captain brought us to our destination—anchored far from a shore in the middle of the small archipelago. Against the current, he could not swim to return to the boat. The Thimble Islands were sharp—like rocky icebergs, they extended mysteriously underwater—and because of this, none of us felt comfortable grabbing the wheel and saving the captain. By another boatsman, the irritated captain was rescued.

For a long weekend, I drove to southern New Jersey to be with friends and family. When I returned, I found our relationship had gone cold—that was all the time needed to lose that sense of romantic complicity with Cyan. Romantic complicity, like being in cahoots about something in which no one else is aware. An unexecuted heist, a criminal left with his plan. Heat transfers conductively through adjacent matter, through fluid in a process called convection, and heat radiates in space—did not radiate far enough during my brief trip—and ultimately, she considered herself hot stuff...and maybe she was. Because of her hubris, she was *astonished* that I didn't try to court her straightaway. When she said, "I'm surprised you haven't asked me out yet!" this was not a nudge as if I was dragging my feet. For her, my withholding was atypical.

Perhaps this was a harsh assessment, but love is a battlefield, ehh? I've been wounded, and I have wounded; but I will tell you what, I am not a casualty! I liked that coffee shop. The shop was a pathway toward establishing a solid social life in Connecticut. I didn't want to complicate my welcome at the coffee shop—because she was like Rachel, the queen of the place. Now, I felt like used coffee grounds. In the aftermath of the battle, Cyan and I still kept in touch. She turned me onto the poet Jack Gilbert. We share his poems from time to time. If you could cycle water through coffee grounds a few times, well, that would be splendid—but one percolation really absorbs all the flavor.

* * *

With foresight, was his action done? Like Lord-feckin'-Polonius from *Hamlet*, was there a method to Hank's madness?[54] Did his recommendation start as a *plan*?

After a period of time spent living in Las Vegas, Suzie moved to Vermont. In the Sin City, she was involved in a toxic relationship with a jealous man. I only saw digital pictures of the man—he looked like an up-to-no-good clubber...an up-to-no-good clubber! Apparently, he was suspicious to a fault; but at first, I considered sympathizing with him—because after all, from afar, Hank and Suzie *were* in contact while she dated this up-to-no-good clubber.

In the Green Mountains of Vermont, Hank was living and loving life. Suzie was a fish that took a long cast; but he sent out the hook with its bait, waited for her bite, reeled, and she made the move. She was an independent woman, of course, but I imagined his persuasion was fairly influential—so, did his recommendation involve a *plan*?

I'm not much into mysteries, and perhaps this upcoming announcement is done too anticlimactically. But together, Hank and Suzie remained a couple...in a committed partnership, evidently. They are a lovely couple that I will enjoy visiting on occasion, at the very least. If I could live a few versions of life, one of them would be in Burlington, with Suzie and Hank as neighbors—who knows, maybe I will live that life one day. Partners make decisions together, big decisions—that's the cornerstone of partnership, a defining aspect. "You should just come live in Vermont!" he suggested to Suzie.

"Yes, I think I will...that sounds lovely," she ultimately agreed.

In Philadelphia, my father was born...it's where his father was birthed, too. This man—my grandfather—had many siblings, and he was the youngest. They were all girls—and actually—they were *step* siblings; my grandfather was the only child born to his mother. She took care of the other children that his father had with his first wife. My great-grandfather's first wife passed away and left my father's aunts motherless...and no one loves you like a mother.

Camillo was the name of my great-grandfather—born in Italy, moved to the United States in the first decade of the twentieth century with his wife and a few daughters. As the first of our lineage in the United States, he settled in Philadelphia—and worked in New Jersey. Down the shore, Camillo was a carpenter that built houses. Coastal dwelling may be instinctive to my family's being—and my apparent fascination with the mountains may not be in accord with our nature. I was vaguely told by my story-telling father that Camillo's first wife tragically passed. Without the essential care and guidance of a mother, she left Camillo responsible for this bunch of helpless children.

Michael Corleone was struck by the lightning bolt of love.[55] From Apollonia's father, he then garnered patriarchal respect and married her with passionate intent that seemed benevolent despite her terrible death—*one hell of an explosion*. Camillo boarded a ship to Italy, and then discovered his own Apollonia—a new love for his life—to be the maternal figure his children needed; a courting conducted with a considerable amount of determination. To be struck by lightning, one best positions themselves by being made of conductive material. Put yourself out there, you know? I like to imagine the growth of this pivotal branch sprouted via charm.

* * *

When I visited Hank at his remote, communal abode in Vermont, we ended the evening smoking cigarettes in the driveway, looking up at the stars once cast by Varda;[56] or maybe they were portholes on the side of a massive ship anchored in the sky. We purchased a four-pack of beer at Lawson's—frigid outside, we stowed the beer in his trunk earlier that evening—now we cracked open a few ice-cold beers to cap the night.

Hank lived at the commune for a short while—and as I write here with the intent to convey chronology, this trip would have been after my experiences with Carolina, the pompous student, after Sky the smiling nurse, too; a trip tucked in before the summer flings shared with Cyan and Elaine.[57] Hank and I were discussing our wedded friends as we smoked, trying to blow portholes of our own to drift up to the night sky as the other spoke. Our friends in committed relationships, marriages even—maybe they committed too soon, and maybe they were missing out on the wildness that this world can offer when you're rowing solo. Why did they do this, we wondered—for Chrissake, what were we missing?

"Carl Magoin seems like he's doing well...you remember Carl's wedding? The hors d'oeuvres at that happy hour, dude, they blew me away!" I said to lighten the subject.

"Hors d'oeuvres? Get out of here with that fancy talk—" he stopped me.

"Appetizers—they were endless, man, like a goddamn Applebee's," I corrected myself. He was right.

"Eating good in the neighborhood...now you're talking! What I won't forget is drinking those damn martinis—you talked them up, man...martinis are the worst. I don't get it—speaking of things I don't understand." Ah, that was a solid smoke ring—there it goes, up, up, up...

I took a little sip of Lawson's, "Phew, now that's tasty, you're spoiling yourself up here, man."

He raised his drink, "To hoping beer is this cold in hell."

In the middle of the discussion, I devised a fleeting theory about who I was looking for in a companion. Deep down this would describe for whom I was searching, but I was continually obstructed by my juvenile behavior, my apprehension to commitment and the ensuing responsibility. To give myself more credit, my lovelessness had been a pragmatic abstention, and courting a woman had not been my primary objective in life thus far. To be more condemning, maybe I once displayed disproportionate humility with my potential partners—I then realized the lower hand afflicted by this diffidence, and then began to maintain an ego, excessively standing up for myself and my independent aspirations...a self-interest that would convolute new relationships.

When a person is narcissistic, they admire themself by definition—someone else comes along and begins to love them, and as a narcissist, they attach to this person because of the person's admiration or desire—but they do not reciprocate love for—and of—the other. Again, the narcissist loves their match only because the match loves the narcissist—like a mirror, intrigued by, attracted to their interest—their favorable perception of the narcissist. When the prey of this unrequited love realizes this, and stops loving the narcissist—well, the whole damn deal unravels, right?

For me and my failures, I don't think that's what the issue was either—too damn self-deprecating to be a narcissist; although a narcissist may denounce oneself in order to garner a compliment—Jesus Christ, this is complicated. Self-love is constructive; anyway, I believe in the power of self-love—be compassionate to yourself before you go loving another. Love yourself, love yourself every day—just not too much.[58]

But alas, I grasped for a way to vocalize this supreme, but elusive attribute I searched for in a companion. I declared, "Hank, when I know she is the one, I will love her so much that I'll want her to be a mother. I'll believe and trust her love because it's felt, sensed...and I'll be so sure of her love that I know she would bestow this promised care and support to her children. Life is a gift, especially when life starts with a loving mother. The children we could make would get to experience her love, too...and that would be such an exquisite gift to have given."

Hank nodded and took a drag, then another; after that, a final drag of his cigarette. His eyes returned from the starry sky, and he looked over to me, "Exquisite—that's not bad, Zeno." With the intense idea, he was a bit taken aback, but pretty much agreed—had no counterargument though he suggested that motherhood was not the chosen path for all honorable women, and that there was a possibility that this criterion might not be actionable, or manifest due to this reality...or something to that effect.

"I'm probably saying this because I've been spending a lot of time out there..." He then added an idea more abstract, more fitting, probably more meaningful...you can be the judge, "...but love's going to come and go like the ocean and its tides...respect and admiration are the core, a place for the ocean—that pulsating feeling people call love—to rove."

Once more, we looked upon the stars—stars cast by Varda...like ripples where our fishing lines met the water. We agreed to call an end to the night, then walked for the door to go inside. Down a hallway we went, passing three bedrooms behind closed doors. His room was small in width, but the ceiling was high. He pointed to the loft—a platform up a ladder—and indicated that this was where I would sleep. "A humble abode," remarked yours truly, glancing around the room.

"My home is outside these walls, not within...you know that, Zeno," he sagaciously imparted. "And this isn't just bric-a-brac, Zeno...these are artifacts, emblems. You'll see." So, to recall I close my eyes, just like exercising my imagination. Behind Hank, I walk through the doorway again...Clothing and boots are strewn on the floor, but that's alright. On his desk, unopened cans of kippered snacks are stacked, next to paper piled manically. Magnets from ski resorts are stuck to his miniature refrigerator...the word "ELK" in black font upon a white oval. From the window, another set of deer antlers hangs. As a poster on the wall, the Milky Way spirals. Dementia, like a black hole in the universe...but not mine. An inflated globe dangled from the ceiling, too...central to this anecdote, I once quipped.

Up the ladder, now in the loft, he laid out blankets—like a nest from a hospitable bird. So, I lay down to rest...in a nest, in this tree, in the woods. Neared oblivion, almost asleep when Hank asked, "Hey, when was the last time you drank breast milk? I bet breast milk is fucking *delicious*." Like a twilight satellite, that's where his mind wandered. I opened my eyes, to the ceiling close above...the stars still shining.

If I am a shooting star blasting off into the universe, perhaps I'll need to stop this roving, turn around, and go back home. Return to my native country—like Camillo—so I can find her there waiting. Like Hank, maybe I will be able to compel some lucky girl to join me from afar. As I take new steps in this journey, maybe one day she will take a step to the same stone...to cross the river, our shared destination. Or am I just a ring of smoke? Go ahead, close your eyes—curl your lips, make a small opening with your mouth, roll your tongue, and blow out a little tobacco smoke. And now—to space, up and away—I will silently drift...just move forward, you once suggested.

* * *

Hank enticed her somehow—though he sounds like an interesting guy, right? Across the country, she moved and became his partner. The natural beauty of the viridescent mountains, alive in the day—the luminescent lake dreaming by twilight—the salubrious air cleansing with every breath—are all graciously offered by the state of Vermont; all at least partially responsible for her stay. I enjoyed most trips to that scenic and exciting area of the country. Well, I enjoyed all trips, except for one that went completely awry.

Cyan and I had a fling in the summer, and shortly after we broke up I began a deeper relationship with a girl named Navy Blue. Our first date was at a brewery where she drank, "I'll have what he's having." I thought that was a cool way to request a drink.

The second date was at a folk festival in New Haven that was headlined by Oliver Wood. While we sat on a blanket, in a field surrounded by a ring of elm trees, I realized Navy Blue had style—a sense for fashion with her legs crossing in patched corduroy pants. The ambient air was cool on the early-autumn evening. She had excellent sartorial awareness, as my father would say—cool, she simply looked cool.

That day, her raiment was perfectly suited for a folk festival; months later, on the evening before New Year's Eve, we dined at a fancy restaurant in downtown New Haven; and again, she dressed well for the occasion. Navy was attractive, probably the most physically attractive girl I ever dated—she looked kind of like a dirty-blonde version of Mila Kunis. When she looked me in the eyes, dressed up on evenings like the eve of New Year's Eve, I actually felt nervous, had to look away and give myself a silent pep talk, "Come on, man, be cool, goddamn it!"

Petite, adorable in appearance and mannerism, and I liked her tone of voice—I pushed her to accompany me in song. We sang "Baby It's Cold Outside." I can still hear her singing, though she was very quiet—especially when surrounded by a group of people. Shy, anxious, she confessed to being. Uninterested, disassociated was how others interpreted her behavior.

But first, I only liked her for her looks. Then she wasn't sure if I was just going to leave her and move back to Pennsylvania. "I have this whole place to myself, why don't you move in when your lease is up?" "I feel like you're just dragging me around to do things you want to do with your friends...you should be planning trips for us!" "Well, I'm not moving to Pennsylvania unless we're engaged..." and "We won't get engaged unless you move in with me first..." and "You have to like my cats, all of them!"

"Even Azalea? She's a real pain in the ass..."

"Yes—no favorite kitties."

I swear she was quickly coming up with problem after problem—confused me to the point where I could not rationalize any of them. I wanted to sort through the issues, because I did not just like Navy for her looks—I just liked her and was at peace with not overthinking why I liked her—I ain't no monkey, but I know what I like. Who knows, I might have even loved her. You know, I'm not twiddling my thumbs up here in New Haven, Connecticut.

The early stages of our relationship should have been easier. We had only been going out for a few months when the first issue arose—and I usually enjoyed solving problems. She told me of her past spats with depression and other self-inflicted disorders. They were sad storylines. So we didn't drink alcohol together often—it would flare up her depression and wouldn't blend well with her medication. I can only recall one time being drunk with Navy. As we were lying in bed, we discussed life and death in the dark of night. "Life is a gift...you don't think so?" She didn't seem to agree. Eventually, I started to realize that she was not embracing the gift.

Navy Blue was much younger than me, so I had to use my imagination. What was I like when I was her age? I outwardly projected the growth she could exhibit by the time she was my age—so, could I express to her my more progressed means to happiness? If she could be happier, or at least strive for happiness, I would do anything she would request—but at first, I did not know that the answer to this latter question was "No, I could not."

> *Because of my pride in wisdom, I walked the Road that every person can walk, and discover what everyone else already knows if they have paid the slightest attention to life. You made me see that the search for happiness is a personal search and not a model we can pass on to others. Before finding my sword, I had to discover its secret—and the secret was so simple; it was to know what to do with it. With it and with the happiness it would represent to me.*[59]

Some individuals are on the high-level quest toward happiness, and some are not. I suppose some people never tried to start the quest or didn't know they were supposed to…Hank skied 130 days in a single winter, his blades covered every square inch of terrain at Arbol de Azucar. I boarded a dozen times and considered myself the Ski King of the Northeast. Reel in the kite of yore, the sick hat he received for this feat was his reward—like Coelho's sword in *The Pilgrimage*—it represented figurative fervor, and the quest he chose toward happiness…a joy of being on a road with fellow passengers, to a shining horizon. And next winter, I'm sure he'll do it again.

* * *

"I feel like you're just dragging me around to do things you want to do with your friends…you should be planning trips for us!" That was the final straw, I guess—dragged her up to one of my favorite places—Burlington, Vermont—the outdoorsman equivalent to a metropolitan's New York City, always something happening. Navy accused me of this the night before our trip's departure. I contended, "No, we are going on a trip together and I'm introducing you to my friends—it's like a 'kill two birds with one stone' scenario."

So, many miles were driven in silence that evening in early March. We stopped at a McDonald's on the way up, but she had no appetite, was too angry or upset to eat. "Goddamn, that is a tasty burger!" Nothing. "Do you want some of this?" referring to a cigarette smoked after I finished the quarter pounder with cheese. On the long route, those were some of the few words spoken. The other words were continuations of the argument from the evening before, oh well.[60]

At Suzie and Hank's apartment, we spent the night. In the living room, the girls were getting acquainted. In the kitchen, Hank and I were catching up. "Is she alright, man? She looks like she might need to poop?"

"She might have to, man—that was a rough ride up."

He bit from an apple, "Want one of these? A fuckin' apple a day, that's what the doctors say—Suzie and I went apple picking a few months ago—I've been on a kick ever since!"

Years ago, on the way to the Poconos, with deer antlers dangling from the rearview mirror...the memory of a fresh apple core sitting in the center console. "How was that apple?" I asked then.

"Keeping the doctor away..." he started. "I was just thinking about that apple before you hopped in actually—was really enjoying that apple and was grateful to be eating it...it's a miracle that trees make fruits. I guess trees care about their lineage like humans...attract animal passersby with a sweet offering—a plump apple, take your pick, then travel a few miles—cross your branches, like crossing your fingers that that animal will shit out your seeds. Not me, man, good try...I'm not eating any seeds."

Why do trees care about their lineage? Is there a cross-species, collective desire to see Earth covered in life? Elsewhere in the universe, we're not aware of a first seed ever sprouting. Like God, maybe humanity will plant an extraterrestrial seed. In Burlington, "Yeah, I'll have an apple...maybe Navy wants one too." We walked into the living room both holding apples.

"Again, with the apples...this guy can't get enough!" Suzie joked.

"What'd the doctor say?" he responded.

"You're starting to sound like a broken record, Hank!" she added.

"That may be true, darling, but at least I'm not a broken record *player*." We were stunned, unsure if this particular fabricated axiom made any sense. He threw the apple in the air, tossed so that his bitemark spun to the rightward horizon.

* * *

Navy did not eat an apple. On that trip to Burlington, she scantily nourished herself. Situated only a few hundred feet above sea level is the town, but the ride through Vermont ascends and descends like a damn roller coaster—maybe her sickness was related to fluctuating elevation. In the lowlands of New England, she was born, was raised, and she even matriculated at Salve Regina University in Newport, Rhode Island.

When I am up in the mountains, I enjoy being at higher elevation. I sense that I think simpler thoughts—but I will not elaborate with any pseudoscience—will just say a lot of this thinking is beautiful, springing from a head up in the clouds. Why do trees make fruit? To spread their seed?

But why do trees find spreading their seed to be so important?

In Bridgeport, Connecticut, at a music venue called Park City Music Hall, Navy and I saw Daniel Donato perform. He created a musical genre he called Cosmic Country. We also saw the Australian Pink Floyd at the Westville Music Bowl, the Infamous Stringdusters at Toad's Place, a Frank Zappa cover band at the Space Ballroom, and Lake Street Dive at the College Street Music Hall in New Haven. My ideas, each of these dates were. Was that not thoughtful? Just the two of us went to those shows—maybe those dates were not extravagant enough.

To do nothing at all, she also preferred. "Can't we just be a couple of lumps on a log?" I don't know, I guess I was just too busy living—maybe I should slow down, allow myself to be bored—would be like mortar to the bricks that are the events of my life, of our life.

"How about we see Danny Donato up in Burlington in a few weeks?" I thought that would be a practical introduction into traveling together—but the train wrecked on dismantled tracks, vanished to the stars. She probably did have to poop. At assessing atmospheric social conditions, my observant friend was very adept.

With the miserable details from that trip, I do not want to bore you. Though maybe I could have stepped up and been a more supportive person, partner. The weekend was an ironic situation really, one of those systematic conflicts—as she was breaking down, letting loose would have resolved her mental illness and salvaged our weekend—she refused to embrace the trip for some reason. This frustrated me, and my frustration made her even more upset.

So, not all of my trips to Vermont were successful; but on that weekend, Navy and I had one brief, cheerful moment. She mustered up the courage to try snowboarding for the first time. On the bunny slope, I helped her get the hang of the sport. I helped her stand. I held her as she began down the little hill with some momentum. Seemingly in control, I let her go and ran alongside her. She fell forward onto her knees, then stomach and chest. I slid down next to her, and we laughed, hysterically. The beginner run was called "Mighty Mite." Navy Blue was the mighty mite.

As time passes, one periodically starts to wonder about the fish they caught in their net—people with whom one tried to establish an intimate relationship. When alone, like an empty glass, one might start filling themself up with thoughts of regret. If they do not have a therapist, or if they want to get on with their life, they have to keep it simple during these reflections. Among all the mornings that followed her sleeping over, not once did she join me at my kitchen table, or living room couch, with a cup of the coffee I brewed. I might have loved her—but I would have loved her with more certainty if she poured herself a damn cup o' joe and joined me every once in a while. She would stay in bed, then pretty much get up and go.

Navy borrowed her friend's snowboard and wintry attire. In all situations, Navy dressed herself with unrivaled sartorial awareness—cute at all times, and her inexperience with the sport made her even cuter, of course. She looked the part of the snow bunny.[61] She was the mighty mite, the snow bunny that entered my life, but she was an unhappy snow bunny.

* * *

Northbound from Stowe, Vermont, I traveled—the furthest steps I'd taken away from home on the continent—where the mountains are lower, more hill-like and rolling, as if one enters into a different domain altogether. With sporadic scents from farmland filling the car, driving with the windows down, left elbow propped up on the open window, warm from the sun shining above and slightly to the west, I listened to the radio, set quietly. On my face, a smile curled. This was a pleasant silence—traveling alone came naturally.

The work trip I just finished was an overall success. I stayed three nights at the resort in Stowe with my philosophical counterparts deliberating electricity policy matters that would impact blissful electricity consumers and rate payers like we were gods. We debated four options—administrative alternatives to the electricity-generating capacity marketplace of the region. On top of the mountain earlier that day, looking out to the sky, I perceived a hand extending two fingers in the clouds. Option two, I will inform the secretary of the committee when I am back in the office.

By plentiful sun, this new land was enlightened. I traveled north to St. Albans, which is also situated on Lake Champlain and above Burlington, as you know; that day's yesterday was overcast, and we thought rain would fall in the late afternoon. Our meeting finished before noon and the self-proclaimed leader of the committee's mountaineering club chose the route. A hike to the chin of Mount Mansfield before the late-afternoon rain.

On the way down—and now coming in for landing—I told the leader of the mountaineering club that I thought our hike was on my top-ten list of all-time hikes. It was stated earnestly, not as an ingratiating remark to a more senior stakeholder. Silently reflecting, a few on the list were southwestern hikes with my father, Observation Point and Angel's Landing at Zion National Park in Utah coming to mind. Mount Monadnock in New Hampshire with my friend Otto, as well. The trips to the Grand Canyon would all take positions on this list that I silently considered.

Hank and I spoke a month before my work trip. If the timing worked out, we would start from Sterling Pond near Stowe, would hike and camp a few nights along the Long Trail, and end our backpacking in Waterbury. Weeks before, the trip's outlook was promising. But then days before, the skipper summoned Hank to sea.

"Fish are gonna be jumping like a kangaroo, man...the captain wants us to leave tomorrow. I'm real bummed—I picked up a solid trail map from a local shop and everything."

"Damn, dude, and I had a blank space set aside in the book...Chapter 8, The Long Trail."

"Fuck," was his remark.

"All good, dude...I'll come up with something. We'll come up with something," I consoled him.

"No, I've been a real flake lately."

"Summertime, gotta get while the gettin's good, as they say," I consoled him once more. This was disappointing. Visions of twilight discussions on the mountaintop quickly vanished. He had been aware of this work for years, kept him updated when writing was back in motion, "I've been working on the book, man."

A month before the trip, I told him, "I'm getting close..."

"Nice, dude, we'll bring some whiskey and glue this bitch together. I don't want you to do all this leaf-raking just to leave them all in a pile."

With sarcastic agreement, I could hear Suzie follow, "Yes, do things all the way, Zeno—don't leave your coat on the chair by the closet." I will—I'm getting close.

* * *

Nothing Hank and I could do about the situation—and from his tone, I figured the multi-day, multi-week nature of his work was straining his relationship with his girlfriend—or was pulling him from the free time of his life, which he would prefer to utilize pursuing adventure. You know, get the heart pumping so you can have a heavy hand with the salt on your salads and steaks.

I could come up with something exciting enough—spilled some ink on dating escapades before—and going at the hike alone might be more symbolic anyway. You know, coming of age with priorities, responsibilities, and such—a lot of ages of discovery in life, not just the transition to adulthood—but I gotta finish this damn book...so that on, I can truly move. Move forward, you suggested.

I brought my backpack gear with me—maybe I could hike up to the ridge and camp at one of the lodges on the mountaintop once the conference was complete. With precipitation in the forecast, I decided against this plan. Earlier in the week,

I reached out to Suzie to see if she wanted to rock climb or do yoga while I was in the area, but she was also out of town. She politely offered her apartment as a place for me to sleep if I was interested—and I was interested, after all. I drove all the way up to northern Vermont, and Burlington was not too much farther. The charm and possibility of Burlington is magnetic, you see. Almost as magnetic as home:

West Chester, Pennsylvania.

When the self-proclaimed leader of the mountaineering club announced the excursion, I told him I would be his goddamn protégé. He led the way, and every time he turned around there was a huge grin on his face. "I *love* Hellbrook," he would say as we approached a waterfall, a scramble, or a slightly more serious climb. Hellbrook Trail, I loved this hike, too.

He worked forty hours per month—not per week—as a semi-retired consultant and was about sixty years of age. I told him that the hike was probably on my list of top-ten hikes. "That's great!" he beamed, while likely thinking that he'd had a hundred hikes that might top this one; patches stitched on his backpack displayed a few of Earth's greatest mountain destinations.

* * *

I drove to St. Albans. At a fishing pier on Lake Champlain, I stopped near a father and son who had their fishing lines set. The boy used a bobber. In the wakes of the lake, the little red bobber popped up and down. In the distance above the boy's cast fishing line, the Adirondack Mountains stood tall. To Burlington, I then steered my vehicle. At the apartment, I arrived and napped on the sofa where Elaine and I slept the previous summer, where Navy and I slept the previous winter. My sleep was poor the night before, which was the third night at the hotel. I don't sleep well in hotels—the conditioned air always feels wet and stuffy. I finally woke up in the middle of the night, turned off the air conditioner, and opened the door to the balcony that overlooked the resort's outdoor shopping mall—should have done that the first evening.

When I woke up on the sofa, I waited for the rain to subside, and then walked to Church Street. I had dinner at a ramen restaurant and drank a beer. When dinner was laid out in front of me, the rain started to come down again—I was glad to be in a town, with a place to sleep that had a roof. I was glad to have friends in this weird town set above the Green Mountains—in a place that feels like a different realm altogether—where I think happy thoughts and meet seemingly satisfied people. With the front windows of the restaurant open wide, I could hear the band playing at the bar next door. I finished my meal and hustled over, so to not get wet. I had a cherished, but not well-concealed, book with me. I just read the chapter in *The Silmarillion* where Tolkien discusses the lands of Beleriand. His prose is phenomenal.

At a high table, I sat. I swear, the band fused the genre of folk with Elvis Costello pop punk—their rendition of "Eleanor Rigby" was fucking fantastic. I sat by myself, and then this highly employable man in his forties joined me. The table had an unblocked vantage point of the stage and was at an optimal distance from the speakers. To my left, there was an open window, mist from the rain outside was felt. In the summertime, this coolness was refreshing. I placed *The Silmarillion* to my right on the table to keep her dry.

In one breath, the stranger told me about five different jobs he had maintained—at a hospital, overlooking the mentally ill, suicidal even—as a security guard at a local bar called Three Needs—a chauffeur, that once had driven the musician Marcus King, who told him a secret he wasn't supposed to tell—but he told me.[62] He told me his girlfriend was going to meet us and bring friends. His girlfriend was a coworker, and she and her friends were nurses. One of them was single, so the situation started to sound like a romantic set-up of some sort. "You know I'm only in town for the night, right?" confirmed yours truly.

He countered with something like, "If there's butterflies, so be it." But there were no butterflies—she was uptight, and the moment the girls arrived the gossiping began—one of their coworkers was too touchy, literally. An exclusive matter to discuss, work gossip—what the hell was I going to say?

Later on, we went to Nectar's, where Thursday night is Reggae Night. I was given a beer, and I brought the drink straight to the dance floor. Jovially occupied, the dance floor was...and I found a space to dance. My secret's the infinity symbol—I trace this symbol with my hips or wave my hands in this formation. Then I do the Egyptian hieroglyphic move after I have worn out the infinity symbol—really can't do the infinity symbol dance move forever, gotta mix it up.

And around midnight, I shook everyone's hand firmly for a round of "nice to meet you's" and left. Like Holden Caulfield wandering around New York City, I was pretty drunk. I walked up Church Street and stopped in another bar, Radio Bean. Like before, the band caught my attention. If I was a fish, I would chomp at a lot of musical worms dangling on musical hooks—and summertime is the fishing season of the musician.

The band on stage consisted of four funky young folks that may have been seniors at the local university. The male bass player wore a damn dress. The female guitarist was very talented and soulful. Leaning on a pole, I thought back to Chaos Thompson, Otto's band at Millersville. I looked around at the crowd, which contained supportive friends, like we gladly were to the locally renowned Chaos Thompson. They really could get us moving. I made fists and began to swing them like so:

$$\infty$$

and then stopped and thought to myself—back at Millersville, when I was their age, I don't think I had prescribed dance moves like the infinity symbol...systematic solutions to matters such as dancing evolve over time.

* * *

Woke up from my nap earlier, I fed the cats at Suzie and Hank's apartment—an orange cat and a black cat—I suppose that was my small fee. I also brought them an established propagation of my jade plant. For about a year, the plant had grown in a shallow plastic container—soon, the plant would need a deeper pot.

Earlier, when I saw option two in the clouds at the top of my hike, I thought about how thankful I was for having completed a successful work trip. I was proud of my contributions

—the conversations I had with my philosophical counterparts were helpful and thought-provoking—I didn't feel like a phony during the conference. Maybe that sounds pathetic, but this highly experienced group was intimidating. The meeting adjourned—I was thankful, proud.

I thought about the energy economics program I completed at graduate school—how that previous career step was a crucial bridge. My thesis analyzed the stakeholder process that I was now a part of—analyzed what these electricity policy stakeholders were talking about, and who was doing the talking amid the so-called "clean energy transition."[63] As I hiked—and thought with my mind in the clouds, and at peace—I reached a greater hot spring of pride which swelled up as I thought of this energy economics degree. I was proud of that accomplishment, too; and the decision to embark on the degree in the first place. In my late twenties, I carved out that experience. Like a tacking sailboat, I smoothly maneuvered a major career pivot. Riding a wave out to sea, my sails above felt full of wind.

I then thought about my father, and how his approach to life and path in life had always implicitly guided mine. To the same graduate school, I went...and got a similar degree, though his coursework was concentrated on environmental economics. On water quality, his thesis was focused. In the 1970s, before he attended graduate school, there had been an uptick in recreational motorboating on Lake Champlain—marinas popping up at the city of St. Albans. This environmental detriment was the motivation of his thesis work.

The work conference was now complete, and I drove north to St. Albans. Hank taught me to raise my gaze, to savor the glorious views bestowed by the mountains. Then, I glanced down from the view of the Adirondacks to observe wakes from a motorboat making a small wave, the kid's little red bobber popped up and briefly submerged. With me, I brought an empty container. At the fishing pier, I squatted down by the water's edge and scooped up a sample of the lake water for my dad...the fat boy.

9

A Poignant Conclusion

Writing a book is a lot like brewing coffee. If coffee is brewed weak, it's difficult to rectify. Sugar does not make the flavor more robust, and tweaking vocabulary does not improve a story. Coffee does not resolve a poor night's sleep, either. Do you remember a hard breakup? How was your sleep? By the time morning comes, my sleepless mind starts to feel like a half-eaten, shriveled-up onion, left in the refrigerator for too long...like a leaf decaying in the woods after a few poor slumbers. So, the time is here—to rake these leaves into a bucket and place them out on the goddamn curb for pickup.

During a hike along a stream in autumn, I watched a leaf alight on the water and float downstream, out of sight. In a relatively short amount of time, the leaf would have turned to mud for the bank or contributed to the floor of the stream. Mud and soil, not an entity of their own. To be grateful for soil is to be grateful to the leaf, the tree, and its predecessors. Like unglorified and undocumented thoughts and streams of consciousness of the past, the leaf decays and becomes a thread in the fabric of soil.[64] You could write a memoir, too, if you'd like...

Alright, so what's the moral of this damn book? Well, maybe you already know—was there a reason you read my book in the first place? Like a Tao, I simultaneously balanced the profoundness within *All About Love* and *The Art of War*—bounded by their covers and on pages just like this one. What messages would you expect to find?

Once upon a time, I bought a jade plant the size of my fist. I still have her—that's right, cutting to the chase with a mawkish metaphor. I used to call the jade plant a rockstar. When I talked *about* the plants in my verdant apartment, I would say, "She's the rockstar"—and when I talked *to* my plants, I would say, "Jade, you are a rockstar!"[65] When I moved westward to State College, I bought her. At around the same time, Hank moved north to Vermont...people gather, and people disperse. And, as you may recall, this was a few months after you and I met and started our relationship.

Hank returned from Aspen, Colorado a day after yours truly. He thought we were all planning on staying there a day longer than we did, so his flight was many hours after mine. At the airport in Denver, he arranged an alternate flight that had a layover in Florida. I worked the Monday that followed that enjoyable weekend out west...and Hank returned to Philadelphia later that evening—at about the time when corporate people like me finished their work. On the beach that day, while consuming frozen drinks, Hank—who was never one to partake in the racing of the rats—greatly improved his tan.

At a local bar on Washington Avenue in Philadelphia, you and I plopped down; and poor Hank, the weary traveler—with his adventure almost cut a day short—met us for a drink. Hank's father was working in the city and joined us there, too. To their house in the suburbs, his father would drive them back. On barstools, you and I sat, facing away from the bar. Dressed in corporate casual attire, the gleeful father stood next to his equally gleeful son. While socializing with Hank and Mr. Bellefonte, you left an outstanding impression. On occasion since, Hank would tell me his dad asked about you—but knowing Hank, that might have been his covert way of seeing if there were any updates involving the two of us. I probed once to see if this was the case; then he confirmed, "No, my dad really did fuckin' *love* her!"

Do you remember that trip I took to Colorado? I was so frazzled about purchasing an extra ticket for the event. Earlier that day, your grandmother died. Like a goddamn child, I had stickers strewn out on the floor when you arrived —stickers collected from a recent beer festival attended in Atlantic City, the beer festival with the stripper dunk tank—and don't anyone forget it. In the early stage of a relationship, it's helpful to be with your potential partner every three or four days, I'd say—breathe the thing to life...like adding kindling to a fire or blowing air on the coals. Before I departed for Denver, you came to see me that prior evening. You were sad, of course. I remember the heartbroken weakness in your embrace, which was a typically strong embrace. Faintly smelling of tobacco, you purchased a pack of cigarettes and smoked a heater on the walk over—the only time I recall you smoking a cigarette.

At that time, we did not know each other abundantly well. But we liked each other, were intrigued by one another, and were on steppingstones above a rolling brook to a surer path of love, on the far bank of the stream. The stream getting deeper, there was seemingly no stone to jump to next—because I had some personal news that I needed to share with you. In a few months, I would be leaving the city to begin graduate school two hundred miles away in State College, Pennsylvania—the happy valley.

Our path became unblazed, I thought. My anxious mind could not see how a relationship would work—you know, I was not sure how the bond of our relationship could grow like my rockstar jade plant. After the trip to Colorado, I told you about my plans with a gloomy, hopeless tone of expression.

...And the next day, you brought champagne to celebrate. With a master's degree of your own, you understood better than I that this enrollment was an excellent opportunity. The academic journey on which I was about to embark would be a major life achievement, a badge of honor—hard to describe the graduate school experience without sounding righteous—and you promised to lovingly, proudly support me as I pursued my personal legend.[66] But what was my personal legend?

That was such a grandiose goddamn time in my life. As a worker, I could change industries, be impactful in the next one that needed my ability and enthusiasm. So I was navigating my career well, I suppose—others stayed on the ladder...where I went up a rung, paced along a moving walkway in an airport to another terminal, jay-walked, rope swung into a river, floated down, and then up a damn escalator—been interesting I guess—jumped around like a kangaroo. Aboard a train, to probably exit through a turnstile gate to my eventually being a dissatisfied American Faust. But one day, another version of myself began walking along train tracks to this story...

With navigating the sea as a partner in a partnership, I guess I haven't been too capable. Man overboard! Navy Blue suggested this—well, she bluntly told me that I was a terrible partner—and by that judgement, I feel haunted. From my vantage point, the partnership you and I once shared was the most significant.

With sincere depth, you're the only person I ever loved romantically.

As I suggested earlier, this string of stories may have seemingly lacked a villain. Mephistopheles was the liaison between the devil and Faust, who desired scientific intellectualism above all, even his immortal soul. I think it was a Cadillac Escalade...the Mephistopheles in the life of your narrator. But all along, maybe I was the villain. I was a Casanova fairly gifted in swooning, terminally disinterested in the authentic, caring service needed for love. When love was an island near in sight, I withdrew—abandoned ship. Now here I am, marooned and glorifying my friend—who I would characterize as an intriguing, genuine person—and genuine, maybe I was the least of all. I stood up to speak my mind, and down I would fall. To some extent, I suppose, Hank and I both preferred to be engaged in unadulterated adventure as shameless lotharios. So, by acknowledging our story and seeking change, maybe we will both become heroes. Heroes that live the change.

Was I a victim? Did I take the bait of individualism—which is characteristic of the American dream—too seriously? Now I am lonely, without a partner—sans S'ville!

Or am I a coward? When the path toward a loving partnership required bravery, I chose a different direction. Yes, like a guitar unstrung, I couldn't ease your pain with affirmation. You departed through a turnstile to a happier valley. I'll find a happier valley, too; carved with time by the storms of an idealist's heart.

When one writes the story of a life in the process of being lived—like I have attempted to do—it seems you could portray yourself as all these types of characters. Labels are much simpler. In a park, along the paved path, the plaques on the benches commemorate these countless figures. Why was I a victim? Why was I coward? Or was I the villain all along?

* * *

My parents are great, I love 'em! They love me, and each other, too; but their love could be imperceivable, not readily apparent. That was my upbringing, where their love was mysteriously displayed. My dad would buy my mother a bottle of bottom-shelf gin for Christmas, but he'd drink two-thirds of the bottle by summertime...and during this season, my ma drank tonic water with a splash of gin on the deck in the sun. So—as an example—the exchange of gifts was not a love language wordlessly spoken between my parents.

You were perplexed by my father—tough nut to crack—and your empathetic work was focused on care for geriatric patients. Yes, the fat boy is strong, but he's getting older. His wisdom, knowledge, and can-do attitude always inspire me, but his stoicism could be confusing. At times, his displeased attitude almost felt unnecessary.[67] That said, he gleaned much from his frugality, attitude, and work ethic. He owns a home down the shore that's a haven from boredom and unhappiness—this is only a dream for many Pennsylvanians. Two healthy fruits, my successful sister and me...a writer, for Chrissake. My dad's writing as well, a screenplay about the Crusades. Like father, like son...you know?

My first tattoos honored my parents. A silhouette of the inventors of the airplane and their glider aircraft—the first project I recall working on with my father was a book report on these brothers. A cup of coffee—representing the communicative relationship I have with my mother. We built a fairly deep, forthcoming space to share our emotions and attitudes toward events and people; as deep as we could go...it may not extend that far down relative to others, but we were always excited to dive together. We were especially content chatting over a cup of coffee in the morning. Discussing morals and hard decisions like playing tennis with an evenly matched opponent—you know, playing tennis against someone who's much better or worse than you is not as enjoyable as an even competition. We didn't necessarily explore unknown intellectual territory—we sort of floated on inner tubes, anchored to a dock on the bay.

Intelligible love, my parents may have displayed—but then a video call altered my perception. My mother joined my sister's group call after I first responded. Lying next to her in bed, clothed and above the covers, was my father—both retired from work, surely buzzing around the house before the call, and now a quick rest in their bed. The visual impression was that they were both just hanging out that way. This glimpse was so simple, sweet to see. But was the relational damage already done? One can really only run water through coffee grounds once...sugar won't change who I am. Was this all a story worth telling?

Penn State is my father's alma mater, too. When I graduated, my parents visited for the ceremony. After the commencement, we went to Madden Cafe for dinner—remember that place? We had dinner at Madden's. Yes, you visited me in State College—just you and me—and we went to Madden's. When you and I were driving back to my apartment from the restaurant, it was snowing, and I got in a minor car accident. At the bottom of two rolling hills, I was stopped and waiting for a car to pass so I could turn left. Behind me, a car was stopped, and then was rear-ended by a damn bus. The driver was delivering cookies. I wonder if those stoned scholars got a refund—maybe they ordered a second batch of cookies and sent another poor son-of-a-bitch delivery guy out into the snowstorm.

After the meal at Madden's with my parents, celebrating my grand accomplishment—which was a few months after you and I decided to break up—my mother handed me a card with a congratulatory and sentimental message scribbled by my father—in block letters he concluded:

USE YOUR HEART FOR YOUR NEXT BIG MOVE

This was a serious suggestion—but the advice also likely referred to a children's movie from long ago, which we watched when I was a child, *Max Keeble's Big Move*. My father really got a kick out of that movie. My parents and I celebrated my graduation. I didn't hear from you—no, we didn't speak much after we split apart...

* * *

We were like a couple of clocks aimed at midnight when we first met. You sat to my left at the bar at 2nd Street Brew House in South Philly. As we talked, your minute hand slowly ticked clockwise, and mine counter counterclockwise, until fifteen minutes later we were facing one another—all hands of the clock...hour, minute, and second—and then, like a flash of lightning on the horizon, you asked me, "Do you like music? Who's your favorite band?"

With honesty, I was reluctant to respond. Most people would raise their eyebrows in mild disgust upon hearing that the answer was Phish. "I'm a crazy Phish guy." You quickly swiveled your chair, and all your hands to midnight, and with both fists you pumped and exclaimed, "Yes! I *love* Phish!" We learned that we were at the same concert at Madison Square Garden in New York City, just a few months before.

Sharing a favorite band was such a pleasant initial common ground. I will never forget that tranquil winter morning—you know which one I'm going to talk about...in the passenger seat as you drove parallel to a winding river right next to the road, surrounded by snow-covered trees with the sun shining through the windows in the beautiful state of Vermont. Close your eyes—do you see evergreen and white? Through the speakers of your Subaru, the Phish song "Roggae" played.

In my life, this was a rare moment. My heart spoke to me like a seductive woman in some foreign language. I sensed I was in love, and that I *could* love—and if I could, I would—you know the rest. I was so pleased and happy, and sensed—was sure—that this was a shared feeling by the adorable, fun, curly-haired girl in the driver's seat. When we crossed the border departing Vermont, en route to Pennsylvania, you whispered back, "I love you, Vermont." Still, those words ring in my head...perhaps that's why I'm so drawn to this lovely part of the country. To cross the border, hear them ring again.

Hank taught me how to inwardly capture views of the mountains with his artistic eye... how to savor views of valleys from above as well. In hearing and feeling the mountains to some extent, I'd be comfortable declaring that my enlightenment came from you. Then, upon my father's guidance, I listened to my heart as often as possible. Across all this time, how and when does one listen to their heart?[68] I can consult with my mind to make decisions. With my mind, I can reason positions, justify ideas that are rational, and condemn the ones that are unjust. Through my career and on my damn adventure, my intuitive mind has guided me. I tried to stay in touch with my heart, too. About a year after graduation—and a little more time since we had broken up—I eventually had to ask a spiritual friend of mine, "How do you listen to your heart if your heart doesn't speak?" She thoughtfully answered:

> *Your heart speaks without words. Like a burning flame, it springs from the anatomic area of your heart. It's a feeling of emotion that is pure and uncorrupted by fear or any ego. Something that makes you smile warmly...a spontaneous "yes" and*

> *a driving force. To listen to your heart, to come to this connection, first requires practice...you need to get to know your heart. Meditation and mindfulness can help...but also self-reflection, self-forgiveness, and compassion. Once you can listen to your heart, this connection is something that makes you excited about life, is not necessarily a rational feeling. It's like a knowing that is calming and peaceful.*

As I mentioned before, you are the judge of this book. If it's not impactful altogether, if this long string of rambling words is not even original, either—maybe her answer above is a worthy and novel literary contribution. I thought her message was pretty damn beautiful. How did it resonate with you?

But when one is as ungifted in the matter of love as yours truly, guidance like this fleets like all the rest. A knowing that is calming, peaceful—my book of realization, like a cloud in the sky—will it never dissipate? Evaporate? Or will it all float away...

* * *

"If I were to write a story, what would I write about?" was what I pondered many years ago, right before I met you actually. Despite the intent to focus on Hank, the story would ultimately be mine. I am writing chapters all alone up here, carving out chapter after chapter, from place to place. I wanted to avoid observing people, businesses, or residences losing their luster. Likewise, I did not want people to witness me lose my glow, my novelty. So I remained on the move, maintaining my sheen like a rolling stone. Like Ken Kesey's Randall Patrick Murphy…gathering no moss. From apartment to apartment, I lugged along my plants. Averse to staying in one place for too long, but where was I heading? How'd you keep your wanderlust at bay? There's a library of stories I could have written. With peace, I should let someone else write them…

If I focused on Hank Bellefonte, I would capture the spirit of my decisions and aspirations—for his valorous adventure thus far was a story of which I only saw or heard glimpses. He shipped out to sea, first driving down to the point of departure. As the captain and crew were procuring provisions on land, they decided, "Eh, instead of provisions for seven days…what about seventeen?" Twenty tons of scallops on that trip, much of which Hank had to lift. When I talked to him on the phone back on land, he sounded exhausted. I failed to persuade him to make a pit stop in New Haven on the way back to Burlington, Vermont.

Newport, Rhode Island—I was there on a work trip. Seated at the table after lunch had been eaten, I rubbed elbows with a heavyset, middle-aged stranger from another company. The meal tired him. "Now I'm sleepy," he said. So I recommended the coffee. He told me about the one cup of coffee consumed in his life…how he took one puff of a cigarette and was disgusted. "Beers?" I asked tersely. He was inebriated twice in his life. "A viceless man," I quickly concluded.

"No, I really like potato chips," finished the gourmand. After the meeting, he probably went up to his hotel room and watched television, for Chrissake. I laced up my rollerblades and explored town. I eventually plopped down at the

Red Parrot. I like sitting down at a bar after doing something that required a lot of physical effort...like I'm a cowboy who traveled many miles on a horse, sitting down at a saloon. So, dare I proudly say, my life has been an adventure, too. I am always grateful when my life converges with ole Hanky Boy, my legendary friend.

One day, Hank will inevitably be an old man. And like a cat, he always lands—he'll land there, too. Yes, we'll be old one day, but these words I've written will be as young as they've always been. When I wrote them, with a relatively young body and mind—and perhaps a young heart, as well—no one could do it better than Hank. Hank chased the horizon, and I chased him.

A ringing phone, "Talk to me."

* * *

J.D. Salinger's *The Catcher in the Rye* was the book I appreciated most, the one I found to be most brilliant. It was hard to resist deploying Salinger's goddamn tone...and I felt compelled to utilize his ultimately surprising framework—the whole book you are thinking to yourself, "What the hell is wrong with Holden Caulfield? This kid is a petulant little jackass..."

Caulfield was the narrator. At the end of the book, he reveals that he was not just speaking to "you," and that he was rather speaking to his beloved deceased little brother. When he was alone, that was what he did, he spoke to his brother. So Salinger cleverly deployed this literary twist. When I realized the whole story was not being narrated to "me" and that the story was a conversation he was having with his departed brother, I understood the source of his sourness and I broke down in tears. I thought, "How didn't I realize that sooner? The kid is completely heartbroken."

When he was a child, Holden loved his brother. *The Catcher in the Rye* was set during his juncture to adulthood. Reluctant to cross that juncture, the bridge of maturation, he acts out because he would prefer to remain a child. Holden does not want to lose his childish spirit, which existed at a time when he had a brother he loved. He preserved his brother like a museum display. Holden did not want to proceed with aging, maturing. He was disinclined to observe any change within himself in subsequent visits to the museum.[69]

On three occasions, I journeyed to the southwest with my father. During the second trip, we pitched up a tent that I bought for crude shelter at a music festival. On the south rim of the Grand Canyon at the Mather Campground, my father and I built fires, ate, discussed our hikes, drank beer, and slept. When we arrived during elk mating season, we found our campsite occupied by two elk that had already staked their claim. The look in their eyes indicated that they were between mating sessions. I swear sexual satiation glowed in the eyes of one elk, while the other elk's eyes and flared nostrils said, "Don't fuck with us." The park ranger let us stay at a different campsite, maybe fifty whole feet away from the mating elk.

On this second journey across the country, I was better acquainted with the windy city of Chicago. I worked there for four weeks in October. On some trips, a traveler may over-pack. But I was under-packed in Chicago. Those walks to the office—toward the end of the work trip, when the wind was whipping—were very brisk. And on the weekends, I wandered. Alone in an unknown city, I roamed, feeding my adventurous spirit, making the spirit greater. At the time, wandering was an affordable approach to experiencing the variety of civilian tones. With anxiousness from perceived danger and peacefulness in safety, a wanderer can feel the spectrum of success and destitution, block by block. When I walked through the doors of stores, I started to feel the pressure to spend, and spend some more. I'm not a shopper. No, I don't enjoy that salesperson pressure to spend. So I mostly strolled along the sidewalks of the city, pondering...

...a wandering memoirist on tracks, approaching a train station, for a ride into the city. The platform is in sight and the train is scheduled to arrive in minutes. So I slow down organically...I'm in less of a hurry to get there. This new speed is in accordance with the desires of my physical being. Such a slow, tired speed...have I been kidding myself this whole time? Am I really exhausted?

Along this way, I acquired useful items such as my damn tent. I gained perspective from work and other life experiences. Between trips to the southwest, I exhibited these noted changes. For Holden, any change he observed within himself was sorrowful. He was, of course, aware his brother had been ripped from the ground. When he revisited the museum, his mourning was magnified.

Spontaneously, my father and I stopped at a state park in Nevada. My father was thinking about his existence and the possibility that he might never come back to this place—well, actually that was what he solemnly worried out loud—so in silence, we mutually contemplated our mortality, appreciated the moment before drifting.

Holden *is* the catcher in the rye. He tries and fails to safeguard other kids from plummeting off the edge while they are playing games in the field of rye. In his interactions, he hopelessly tries to prevent classmates from growing up—like falling off a cliff when you are gleefully playing tag in a field of rye with your friends. Because of his understandable repulsion to maturity, Holden challenges his peers as they approach the next phase of their lives. He indoctrinates his little sister—culminating in one of the book's final questions:

> Will they run away?

The very second that I closed the book, I tossed it on the table and called my sister to discuss all these ideas. Still, when I think about *The Catcher in the Rye,* I get teary-eyed—never fails. Brilliant book by a genius—takes one to know one, eh? I wonder how this analysis matches up with the book reports of countless teenagers. You read it when you were in school, right? That's what every son of a bitch says when I ask them if they read *Catcher in the Rye*.[70]

* * *

Walking on train tracks alone through the woods, like writing a memoir. Approaching a station at last—a few pages left, just a few words left to write—soon I'll join with the road and walk my sorry ass home, with cars passing by me.

Yes, coming in for landing with the final metaphor. The jade plant, I sure enjoy taking care of her—she still is the rockstar. With plant supervision, I try not to wait until the pot has been outgrown. Growth is sometimes clear and visible; but, of course, there are roots below the surface. In the soil, the roots may start bunching up against the terracotta. When the time comes, I try my best to gracefully re-pot a plant for continued growth. Acknowledging and maintaining this type of growth is probably more of a detached process. But still, plant care involves will. One must say to themselves, "I want this plant to live." I am growing…and we were growing, too. Yes, for me, upkeep involved in partnership has proven to be trickier.

I was so fixated on my personal growth. As if our root balls could not have intertwined—as if that would have restricted my intellectual development and position in the world. We could have been two transplanted flowers growing in the same pot. Self-love along the way, like ensuring soil is nourished with nutrients and such. Here and now, I honor the soil we could have shared. I honor the self-perpetuating tree we could have been. I admire the forest, a community of life and love. Life's a gift…and what a beautiful gift when given through love. I guess I learned too late. Were you the right person at the wrong time?

You gifted me a pothos plant that is still alive and doing fine. I went away somewhere and left my plants with my mother. She left the pothos plant hanging outside one night. That evening, the temperature dropped significantly, and the plant nearly died. I salvaged a few tendrils. Altogether, there were maybe ten leaves in fair condition. Today, atop my refrigerator, the pothos plant lives. She's here in New Haven, Connecticut. Soon, I will have to re-pot her again. I began propagating tendrils and building a new bundle in a different pot altogether.

With neglect, plants droop, wither, and die. Like the poor aloe plant, which did not endure as well. With care and recognition, this all can be prevented.

As a failure seeking vindication, I opine that love is a bold act. One of my final observations is that love is the boldest and bravest act of all. Parenthood may be the most dutiful; but loving intimately, the boldest. Humility is a part of my charm, engrained in my being—maybe humility became my curse as well. One day I will have to be bold like others—what I always lacked, and what was needed with you. Words of affirmation, shout from the rooftops. I was caught up in my own ecosphere. I was also intrigued by the world of women, worshipped the endless sea. After all this writing, will I have done what I set out to do? Will I reach the shore, to instead become a woman's world? Then the world could perhaps become ours and we'll find other things to worship.

If I were to have the audacity—or the madness—to write a book, I once pondered about the book's focus, the motivation of the story. The contents of the story themselves could be heroic adventures—and could involve the short-lived, romantic escapades of a few thrill seekers; one who arguably sought excitement and pleasure of a much higher degree. Could the act of telling you this story be heroic, chivalrous?

If our escapade was longer lived, an eternity if time permitted, what would have become of this so-called adventure? House blend instead of French roast? Would I have used the right ratio of coffee grounds?

If I told this story, what's the next book I would live? I wondered this, too.

Now you might understand at last—rather than declare out loud, I will type like the coward I tend to be. None of these other women on the easel that paints the sea ever matched the kindness and inner beauty that you showed to me. Hard articulating this stuff, better late than never, they say. They also say some things are better left unsaid—who are they, and what are these things.

I will say them anyway. I'm sure your life will be wonderful. At this time, I wish for your life to be wonderful. If you would rather life not be so damn wonderful, I hope you proceed happily. Like a swan with a partner in a calm pond...not navigating a vast sea with a horizon always out of reach. If I became a villain and broke our hearts, and you would rather me not hope for anything at all...well, seems it's too late—and I apologize for this, too.

Detaching from our final embrace, my visceral being shouted out, "What the hell are you doing!?" Simultaneously, my mind was like, "Listen, that's your heart talking...your heart!" It was a goddamn code red. So this all has been like an incident report of that day; a synopsis of my mistake, a dissertation on that chapter of life.

You know how your ears hear one string of words, but another string is spoken? A phrase that is misheard and misconstrued is a mondegreen, you might recall. "I hope you fall in love with New England," were the last words you spoke to me. Wounded with a hot bullet to my being, I heard, "I hope you fall in love *in* New England." If you had a therapist or a helpful friend, they probably instructed you to conclude our relationship with a meeting marked with finality. When we met that day, I still loved you. Now, a lot of days I feel as dumb as a damn pin ball.

Plenty of fish in the sea, and I am done being the ball knocked around—but I turn a city corner, and there is a cute girl waiting for her dog sniffing a bush. Pow! Right between the eyes, I am filled with excitement—to chase a girl that probably does not want to be chased; obsessed with the hunt. *"Players only love you when they're playing"* always felt like an indictment, not an observation in lyric. So, underneath my charm, I am starting to see my fault. *"When the rain washes you clean, you'll know."*

So, what am I going to do now that I have admitted my wickedness? Who the hell knows—right person at the wrong time, I tell myself. I will care for the pothos plant anyway, and look forward to the next one she creates, too. Your love was a gift. I won't take love like this for granted if there is a next time.

So, I am at my desk. I am getting close to the end. I am submersed with all of this personal discovery that I would like to last. On this writing excursion, I set out to honor my friend. All along, I also wanted to resolve why I am the way I am. I figured the former would be more scintillating, tantalizing to a reader.

And my book became my close friend, you see. My real friends infrequently solicit my thoughts on their relationships, and I rarely seek their advice either. My sister, my confidant, is now a mother—she helps, but she has a lot going on...

In the playing field, the battlefield, the park and forest,

there are a lot of simple and straight men like me wandering on their own. So I wrote a book. If my book were a friend, he would ask, "So, Zeno, you've already been quite pretentious despite your sister's advice...but be as sentimental as you would like anyway—how should you move forward?"

She loved me.
She gave me a pothos plant,
Which still pours out tendrils like love.
I take pride in the health of the plant.
She had to move forward,
But she once gave me the gift I seek.
Tend to the pothos plant, my sword.
Keep her close to the sun.
Next time, I will accept the gift of love.
By loving a partner intimately,
Boldly, and bravely.

In my glove compartment, you discovered a set of feminine eyeglasses. Angered, it was like I had been storing a prize. *He then wedged the photograph back in the clip, took another coffee sip, and we proceeded with our trip.*

I don't know exactly what to do with this little piece of treasure stored in my desk drawer. Notes you wrote to me, a picture of us from the time you straightened your curly hair. At Boathouse Row in Philadelphia, we dressed up and attended a party. Such a joyful picture, and now I don't want your shining smile to vanish, fade way...

Your smile was a gift, too. Like that first pothos plant, I will eventually have to hold on to you some other way; ensure you live forever, subliminally. I'll propagate the tendrils of the love you once bestowed and use them when I become that lucky girl's world.

I remember seabirds flying across a grey sky, above a still carousel. Through a misty veil, I remember this—like a motionless object in a museum, we quickly passed by these painted horses before we found refuge from the rain at a wharf restaurant in Boston, Massachusetts. With college football televised in the background, we drank beers and ate delicious clam chowder. This scene is a cherished memory through a misty veil that's getting foggier.

Hopefully all these words will be like seeds in soil. With any luck, one day there will be flowers around my home. Though while it may not sound highly foundational, a home with wheels may be more grounding for a person like me. I could renovate a van—a modified and mobile home outside the confinement of a property, not within...convert my wanderlust into wander-love. I don't feckin' know.

Either way, I thank you,

To whoever reads this book, please give yourself some credit, too. You have reached the end! If this were a movie, upward your name would go, like a hot air balloon taking flight—off the screen to the song "A Life of Illusion" by Joe Walsh. Give it a spin!

In the Bible, Isaiah says, "Behold, all you who kindle a fire, who equip yourselves with burning torches! Walk by the light of your fire, and by the torches that you have kindled! This you have from my hand: you shall lie down in torment."[71] But to get here—to the end of this goddamn book—I first turned inward to my mind, often turned to the burning fire wavering through the weather of life, and I consulted my heart and soul within the flames—and I asked:

"To whom would the book be narrated?"

or rather,

"Well, who would you want to read your book?"

and,

"...would the book have a punchline?"

Notes

1. This as is in *writing a book*. Please, for the love of God, do not disregard these notes. There's seventy-one! Although if not too late, this note, I suppose, I recommend disregarding.
2. I am not sure if I do—something about the context strikes me as misogynistic—but no turning back now...if I say the wrong things, I apologize.
3. (speculation as well)
4. Many thanks to the card's true personage, whose likeness helped us dupe the eyes of the law on a tri-weekly basis.
5. *Cat's Cradle* by Vonnegut contains a chapter about indexes. "Flattering to the author and insulting to the reader" is one remark regarding an author's own addition of an index. I will refrain.
6. Perhaps your narrator has an anger issue—be vigilant, he might not be the benign narrator you hoped for. Though in college, sometimes people got kicked out of parties—and for someone to get kicked out of a party, someone else has to be a kicker.
7. From the Bible
8. Bodega consisted of recent graduates from our high school who were then students at the University of the Arts.
9. From *Pulp Fiction*
10. From *All About Love* by bell hooks
11. Paying homage to Kurt Vonnegut—though I am not a "Vonnegut guy." Someone asked me this once, "Are you a *Vonnegut guy*?" No, I am not a Vonnegut guy—but I did read *Slaughterhouse Five*, *Cat's Cradle*, and *Breakfast of Champions*. Solid books...
12. During my freshman year, I lived with a stranger. Then, as

previously shared, I lived in an apartment with Wayne, Angelo, Otto, and Smitty the following two years of school. For a change of scenery, we disbanded—Wayne, Otto, and Smitty rented a home near the House of Pizza. Angelo and I moved in with Carl to a home in E-Courts. From the trash, our couch was picked. Like a hyperbola, our terrible television displayed. The edges of the laminate floor swelled from the absorption of spilled beer.

13. ...or perhaps a therapist. If this book does not sell, maybe I could give it to a therapist to fast-track the process—a penny saved, a penny earned.
14. Imagine hearing "Walking on the Moon" by the Police during this upcoming scene.
15. *Caddyshack*—as if the character played by Bill Murray is the persona Hank embodied.
16. *Mutability* by Percy Bysshe Shelley
17. Shelley's clever deification of the spiritual being that permits one to fall asleep.
18. "I was feeling oh so bad, asked my family doctor 'bout what I had."
19. About this matter, I presume Chaz would have no issue with me being forthright.
20. I still think the internet web page was defectively constructed.
21. God, I wish I never trusted that process.
22. From *Nine Stories* by J.D. Salinger
23. Do you remember those Pokémon balls?
24. From *The Silmarillion* by J.R.R. Tolkien
25. Kindly refer to Chapter 2—or recall the nutcase who ate the flies.
26. *Frankenstein: or, The Modern Prometheus*
27. Tectonic activity was likely more consequential, but this seemed cogent at the time.
28. I went backpacking with someone overly concerned about bears. I get it, precautions are necessary—but leaving a concealed fruit snack package on the table struck me as low risk.
29. Reference to Ken Kesey and the Merry Pranksters
30. "Theme from an Imaginary Western" by Jack Bruce—next up on the soundtrack.
31. In the back of the book, there's a picture of Hank from the Après

in Aspen taken by yours truly. Isn't he the grandest of the bosom revealers!
32. *"Try to find heaven in hell, found a haven right here"*—catchy lyrics by The Growlers
33. Though the love displayed in *The Sandlot* between Wendy Peffercorn and Squints may be a close second.
34. Yes, a couple of quotes from *Pulp Fiction*.
35. Acknowledging privilege is important—my degree from Penn State University may be my utmost privilege.
36. *The Pilgrimage* by Paulo Coelho
37. *Jaws* by Steven Spielberg
38. From *The Art of War* by Sun Tzu
39. Did you watch *Eternal Sunshine of the Spotless Mind*? Most of the crying in my life has occurred while watching that movie…
40. "Women are praised and rewarded for being nice, agreeable and accommodating, which makes it more natural to ignore our [their] internal signals to act otherwise." I read this excerpt from *Loving Bravely* and cringed. Writing this book took a while, and I would return to bolster an idea after little moments of inspiration like this excerpt. I felt ashamed that I favored a common gender narrative for her description—very possible this book is littered with misogyny. A flawed, outdated misogynist in progressive times may be the unfortunate backdrop of my story; I suppose it is the theme I am trying to resolve.
41. Lyric from the song "Cavern" by Phish
42. As a naturalist, he took particular issue with matters such as vaccine mandates and offshore wind energy development.
43. Prior to completing this book, I regrettably never saw him kayak whitewater rapids—God knows I would not be able to participate in that activity—but to get a digital glimpse like I did, direct yourself to the internet and find him as a featured adventurer on the *Why We Go* promotion series by Hydro Flask.
44. From *Chronicles: Volume One* by Bob Dylan
45. Holy shit!
46. "And all night long, amongst these radiant brocades, with her hair hanging loose, divine in her nakedness, she seemed like the goddess he had always imagined who had finally drawn him close

to her immortal bosom and soared with him in a deep and great celebration of love upon golden clouds." From *The Maias* by Eça de Queiroz

47. *The Silmarillion* by J.R.R. Tolkien
48. Kurt Vonnegut calls alcohol "yeast excrement" in *Breakfast of Champions*.
49. That's what this writing business is all about—clever ways to transition between ideas. I am starting to get the hang of this shit and I will tell you what, I am deeply enjoying the writing activity. If you have gotten this far, I am sincerely thankful for that as well.
50. "I know there are other people out there, and other relationships I could create, but I choose this one." From *Loving Bravely*. One of many significant others seems less significant—but maybe it could be more, what the hell do I know—or maybe somewhat significant is all one desires if they are a transient person living in a transient place.
51. Kindly refer to Chapter 1.
52. *The Silmarillion* by J.R.R. Tolkien—apples to oranges
53. From *Friends*
54. "Though this be madness, yet there is method in 't."
55. Michael Corleone from *The Godfather*—imagine the Italian courting sequence of the Francis Ford Coppola film, or the novel by Marlo Puzo.
56. *The Silmarillion* by J.R.R. Tolkien
57. Sorry, I've been all over the place...this book probably could use an index and a goddamn timeline. Kindly refer to Note 5.
58. "We must know, understand, and love ourselves with such devotion and ferocity that the love of another serves as an extension, a mirror, and a validation of that love." From *Loving Bravely*. Maybe love's like one of those mirror mazes at a carnival?
59. From *The Pilgrimage* by Paulo Coelho
60. How about the word "word"? Do you think there were words before the creation of the word "word" that had yet to be classified as words? What were they? Did they have a name? If Navy Blue and I were on better terms that evening, well, we had plenty of time to discuss such matters.
61. Ski jargon for a cute, inexperienced female skier or snowboarder

62. The song that Marcus King was listening to when he lost his virginity
63. If one is politically interested, they may call that what they'd like (e.g., revolutionary, expensive, an eye sore).
64. I will offer a few reasons to be grateful to soil: the green lawn surrounding your home like a halo, the park that brings joy to children, the field for competitive sports. Presently, soil is an analogy to a foundational mesh of mindfulness for any realization —unarchived but inspiring, nonetheless.
65. She's bashful, will probably blush if she gets around to reading this bit.
66. Like Fatima from Paulo Coelho's *The Alchemist*
67. He is a hard man to explain—I'm sure I am, too.
68. Lighting strikes maybe once...maybe twice.
69. Sorry if I spoiled this classic book, but if you prioritized reading this over that, well, that's your goddamn problem—but seriously, I apologize if this is the case.
70. Please excuse my attitude once more—one last fictitious embodiment of Holden Caulfield—been a damn pleasure.
71. Jack Gilbert's *The Great Fires* is also worth a read.